SURVIVAL

STORIES BY NANCY LORD

COFFEE HOUSE PRESS :: MINNEAPOLIS::1991

Some of these stories first appeared in the following magazines: "Imitations" and "The Winner," *High Plains Literary Review;* "Marks," *Antioch Review;* "The Lady with the Sled Dog," *Chariton Review;* "A Guy Like Me," *Greensboro Review;* "Visqueen Winter," *Green Mountains Review;* "The Bucket of Mice," *Alaska Quarterly Review;* "Waiting for the Thaw," *Ploughshares;* "Nature Lessons," *Sonora Review;* "Why I Live at the Natural History Museum," *Other Voices;* "Snowblind" and "Small Potatoes," *Passages North.*

The publisher thanks the following organizations whose support helped make this book possible: Elmer L. and Eleanor J. Andersen Foundation; The Bush Foundation; Dayton Hudson Foundation; Honeywell Foundation; Jerome Foundation; Minnesota State Arts Board; Northwest Area Foundation; Pentair, Inc.; and the National Endowment for the Arts, a federal agency.

Coffee House Press books are distributed to the trade by Consortium Book Sales and Distribution, 287 East Sixth Street, Suite 365, Saint Paul, Minnesota 55101. Our books are also available through all major library distributors and jobbers, and through most small press distributors, including Bookpeople, Bookslinger, Pacific Pipeline, Inland, and Small Press Distribution. For personal orders, catalogs or other information, write to:
COFFEE HOUSE PRESS
27 North Fourth Street, Suite 400, Minneapolis, MN 55401.

Library of Congress Cataloging-in-Publication Data
Lord, Nancy.
   Survival.: stories / by Nancy Lord.
       p.   cm.
   ISBN 0-918273-84-6: $9.95
   1. Alaska—Fiction. I. Title.
PS3562.0727S87   1991   90-27025
813'.54—DC20   CIP

Contents

for my parents

Survival

They say she must have been crazy.

Suicidal, they say.

Self-destructive.

Absolutely nuts.

They shake their heads, in sadness and in wonder. She was not one of us, really, so there is more wonder than sadness. Our people—they go down with fishing boats, plow airplanes into the ground, spin cars off icy roads. They shoot each other, over stolen horses and lost affections. Such deaths are not uncommon in Alaska. We expect them, as we expect snow-choked roads and cabin fever. While we dread and regret them, we know how to mourn them.

Down at the Waterfront Cafe, those who gather for coffee sit slump-shouldered. They're saying this and that, saying what they know, what they've heard. They do this every morning, talking over the council meeting, the weather, the price of bait. They refill their own cups, leave generous tips. This morning, they do more than the usual amount of head-shaking. It is a shame, yes. It was stupid. They want to be angry. What did she think? How could she?

There is only one answer. It is all over town by now—in the grocery store and the bowling alley, on telephone wires between kitchens, on the docks and in the cannery. My neighbors say it; my friends say it; Jim, who might know better, says it. She was crazy, or she wanted to die. It amounts to the same.

How do I know this? I'm not in the Waterfront or any of those other places. I'm on the beach, walking, by myself. The tide is out, just turned, and it leaves a line of foam where it rolls onto the sand. Farther out, the chop tosses the surface of the bay into cut glass. The sun is bright but somehow distant. It's August, and already we're moving away from summer. The snow has retreated up the mountains as far as it will go, leaving bare the hard-blue glaciers that fill the valleys. My eye rests at the peak of the mountain we know as Big Rock. I follow Big Rock's ridge down one side, all the way to tidewater. It ends at Tuskatan Cove. The mountains throw their shadows over Tuskatan Cove.

But how do I know what people are saying in town? I know because I know them so well. I am, after all this time, one of them. When I was twenty, a skinny girl from Minnesota, I had the great romantic notion that I wanted to live in Alaska. I came and stayed, and now it's been eighteen years, all in this same town. Eighteen years! I must like it here, I tell people when they ask. I do like it. And I know how people—we—are. I know how everyone talked when she was missing. And I know how they talk, and what they think, now that she's been found.

Last summer, in June, Bonnie came to town. She hired on at the cannery. Everyone does, initially or eventually or even, like me, regularly. It's mindless work, but at least it's work. You don't live in a small Alaskan town for the job you can get; you do whatever job you can in order to be able to live in such a place.

We were processing shrimp when Bonnie started. I looked up and there was the forelady with a new girl on the other side of the conveyor belt. Etta, the forelady, started showing her how to sort through the shrimp that came along the belt, to pick out the pieces of shell. Etta shouted to me. "Sarah!" She pointed to the new girl. "Bonnie." She pointed back and forth again, introducing us to each other. It's so noisy on the shrimp line, that's about as good as anyone can do for talk. I smiled and nodded. I understood that Etta was instructing me to keep an eye on the new girl.

I took to Bonnie right away. Most of the girls – the college kids up from the Lower Forty-Eight – don't take their work very seriously. They're just there to make some money and say they worked in an Alaskan cannery. Bonnie was different. She leaned intently over the belt, peering near-sightedly at the shrimp and scrambling after the bits of shell as though her life depended on it. She was a large girl – not fat, but big-boned. Bovine, I thought, and then wanted a better word. Strong, sturdy, gentle, and somewhat awkward, as though the child inside were still growing into the larger body.

I tried to catch her eye, to reassure her. She needed to relax, straighten her back, adopt a pace she could keep comfortably for a two-hour stretch. She should have watched my hands, how I flicked my fingers with an economy of motion, how I let some of the shell get past me. We were not the end of the line; more hands had to do their share before the clean shrimp spilled into boxes.

She never looked up. I kept glancing back and forth from the shrimp to her face, kept getting stopped at her eyelashes. They were long and pale and feathery, a lighter red than her hair. Her fiery hair was tucked into a regulation hairnet, the kind the cannery gives out and that no one wears after her first day. They're too ugly, and we're all vain enough to replace them with scarves or hats. Bonnie's hairnet was pulled down low, the black elastic crossing her forehead like a thick frown line.

One strap of her apron kept falling down, and Bonnie kept jerking it back up onto her shoulder. It was not a good apron: an old, short style that didn't fit anyone very well. It was Bonnie's by virtue of her newness. For now, she had the last pick of clothing, but as soon as someone quit, she'd move up to something better. All of us had passed that way before her, paid our dues. My own first weeks at the cannery, so long ago, stuck more clearly in my mind than all the intervening years of seasonal work. I could picture my first apron – torn at the bottom so that it funneled water into my boots. I remembered salmon eggs spilling like jewels, frost billowing from the freezer, the furious sound of fillet knives being sharpened. I'd watched the other women move easily through their tasks and joke with one another, and then they'd joked with me, as though I'd always been there, and I'd felt glad to be a part of them. I could still recall those moments, at the end of the night shift, when I walked out into sunlight and my weariness magnified the glow of the water and mountains, the rustle of a raven's wings as it flew past, so that this corner of the earth seemed even more beautiful than before I went into the cannery, and made my heart ache.

I looked again to catch the new girl's eye, but she was still watching her hands. She was thinking about something, though. I could tell, from the way the corner of her mouth was tilted. She was thinking about something outside the cannery, away from her fingers picking at shell, and that was good.

At her age, I'd been so full of dreams. Alaska, the summer I discovered it, was all I wanted it to be: a land of light and flowers and adventure. I was going to climb every mountain, pick berries beside every bear, raft every river, drink whiskey with every old sourdough. It was like being in love; everything was possible.

Lunch break came, and we all trooped out to shed our aprons and wash our hands. In the locker room, a large green backpack leaned in one corner, a sleeping bag and pad strapped to it. I went on through to the lunchroom and sat with the others.

Bonnie didn't come in, though. I watched the doorway, and then I looked out the window. There she was, standing on the dock, hands thrust into her sweatshirt's pouch and her hair drifting back over her shoulders. She was staring out across the bay, at the mountains and the clouds. The sun was breaking through clumps of clouds, forming a mosaic of different shades of green on the mountainsides and, higher up, lighting the snowy peaks with a brilliance that was almost blinding.

It was noisy in the lunchroom, with everyone talking at once. The smell of coffee barely cut the more powerful odors of fish and chlorine.

I took my sandwich and went outside.

Bonnie didn't notice me at first. Her attention was with the gulls. They were shrieking and flapping, fighting over perches on the dock pilings. One no sooner set itself down and folded up its wings than another shoved it aside, only to be bumped off by a third. Then the first gull went on to challenge another. Except for two mews, the gulls were glaucous-wings; most were immature, their plumage as dusky as if they'd been playing in a coalbin. "Musical chairs," I said.

She looked at me then, as though recognizing me for the first time without my apron. "Oh." She smiled, a shy smile that hid her teeth. "Musical chairs, that's perfect." She went on watching the birds.

I sat down against the building and unwrapped my sandwich.

"Did you bring a lunch?" I asked, ready with advice about the relative edibility of what was available from the vending machine.

She came over and flopped down near me, pulling a plastic bag from the front of her sweatshirt. She took out a hunk of cheese and a package of crackers, then wrestled a Swiss Army knife from her pocket. The knife was attached to a braided lanyard, exactly like the ones I'd made as a child, every year at summer camp, from flat strands of plastic. I hadn't seen or even thought of those lanyards for a quarter century or more, but all of a sudden I could *taste* the plastic. I remembered how I'd used to chew the ends of the strands, turning them sideways in my teeth. The thought somehow made Bonnie seem very young—a new camper, proud of her equipment, excited, prepared.

We both watched the gulls. Bonnie's face was lifted, shining, as though she thought they were fascinating. She broke off pieces of cracker and tossed them out on the dock. The gulls flapped down to investigate, fighting more for the right to do so than for the crumbs themselves. They were all too well fed to care about cracker crumbs.

I thought about telling her that we didn't encourage the feeding of gulls. They were nuisance birds. The more they were fed, the more numerous they became, and the more they crowded out the other birds, proper seabirds like puffins and cormorants.

But Bonnie was enjoying them, so I let it pass. Instead, I pointed out the mew gulls and the difference between the mature and imma-ture glaucous-wings. A tern dipped low over the water and then circled above us, its forked tail tilting like a rudder. "Arctic tern," I said, waving a hand at it. It flapped its wings and headed across the bay.

"It's *so* beautiful," Bonnie said.

I nodded my agreement. "Are you new in town?"

"Yes," she said. "New in Alaska. I need to be here. Do you know what I mean? I need to be somewhere that hasn't been paved over yet. Over there—" She was staring across the bay, as though she was still following the tern's flight. "–over there you could get right down to the essence of life."

What I knew about the far side of the bay had as much to do with rain and mosquitoes as with life's essence, but I liked Bonnie's enthusiasm, her certainty. Essence. The essence of life is . . . I imagined it as a multiple-choice question on a radio quiz show, but I drew a blank on any of the possible answers.

"What do you think you'd find?" I asked. "What would you look for?"

She took a minute to answer, then the words came slowly, thoughtfully. "Just exactly what's there. In nature. On its own terms. Like birds flying. That's what you'd have. Birds. Flight. Birdness. That's what I mean."

Not names, then. Not mew gulls, glaucous-wing gulls, arctic terns. Not labels, but the things themselves. I took another bite of my sandwich. Not a halibut sandwich, but foodness, energy. I liked the concept, in a way. It was so simple, so innocent. It was ridiculous in its simplicity, of course, but young people were allowed that. I hoped Bonnie would be able to hold on to some of her purity of vision, always.

A couple of evenings later, Jim and I sat at my kitchen table and ate ice cream. Jim's a fisherman, as migratory as the fish he chases through Alaska's waters, but as soon as he gets to town I know I'll find him at my door, bearing a dripping garbage sack of undersized halibut or incidental cod. I'm always happy to see him safely on land, and then I'm always almost as happy when he returns to the boat or his own ramshackle house. Jim, with his kitchen takeovers and tales of high-seas disasters, wears me out.

This time, he was telling me about a boat that rolled over in the inlet, and how one of the crew had just escaped getting caught in the rigging. I leaned my forehead against my fist and tried not to picture a line twisted around a foot, dragging an orange-coated figure down through the silt-laden darkness, leaving a path of bubbles streaming up behind, and then bubbles breaking on the surface, and then no bubbles, just the gray sea pitching waves into one another.

Jim bumped his knee against mine. "So what's new with you, Ms. Potatohead?"

Nothing much was new with me. I'd ordered a new set of wheels for my garden cart. At the cannery, we'd been told to expect lots of overtime when the sockeye run started. I mentioned Bonnie, the new girl who'd arrived on her own, all the way from upstate New York.

"She makes me feel old," I said.

"You *are* old," Jim said.

Jim likes to tease me about my age. I'm two months older than he is, which is all he means by it. This time, though, he must have sensed that I wasn't in a mood to be teased. After a moment, he said, "Of course you're not old. Why would she say that?"

"She didn't *say* anything. We were just talking about the other side of the bay. She wants to go live there. I realized I haven't even *been* across the bay for a couple of years. I haven't seen a sea otter or heard a waterfall."

Jim stirred his ice cream. I could tell he wasn't keying into what I was saying. He knew the other side of the bay in terms of where the salmon schooled up, where halibut lay in deep holes, where rocks would tear up a net. He didn't understand the lure of just plain wildness, the idea of going to a place because it was good for the soul.

"Bonnie wants to get down to the essence of life."

Now that I'd said it myself, out loud, I wanted to laugh. What did Bonnie think she knew about the essence of life? Would she recognize it if it bit her on the butt?

"Great," Jim said. "It sounds like a perfume."

"She's so innocent," I said. "Young. I guess that's what it is. There's something about her that reminds me of myself, or of someone I used to be, or thought I wanted to be."

Jim looked at me as though I'd said I used to be an elephant. We hadn't known each other when we were Bonnie's age. When I was new in Alaska, he was busy fleeing in the opposite direction. After growing up in Ketchikan, he'd wanted nothing more than to hit the beaches of California. He'd come back after a few years. Not enough room to take a piss, he always told people, and then would follow with a story about being arrested for taking one behind a tree in Oakland. Somehow, we'd ended up having mutual friends, and then being friends, and then lovers, but neither of us seemed to be the kind to want to absolutely settle down, to merge households and pocketbooks and dreams. We were content just as we were, being able to come together and then go apart.

"I don't know," I said. "Maybe I've just been in Alaska too long."

"Where would you rather go?"

"Nowhere. That's the problem." I couldn't imagine myself back in Minnesota, or Seattle, or Hawaii, or anywhere else, really. "Here she is," I said, tapping my finger on the tablecloth, "sitting on the dock and thinking sea gulls are terrific birds. And clouds. She gets excited looking at a cumulus cloud. And what do I see? Scavengers and rain."

I looked up at Jim, not at his face but higher, at how gray he was getting above his temples. I wondered if he was thinking the same about me—there's Sarah, turning gray. He probably thought I wanted to be twenty again. But I didn't want to be twenty again; the very idea made me feel tired. I just wanted not to forget that feeling of having the whole world bright and new, that way of seeing birds before they had names, of knowing so definitely that what was important lay in the land and how one lived with it.

Jim reached across the table and took my hand. "You're all right by me," he said.

I left my hand in his but didn't return his squeeze. Jim was doing his best, but all right wasn't what I wanted.

Every morning Bonnie arrived at the cannery with her pack; every evening she hiked off with it again to pitch her camp somewhere in the trees. Somedays she smelled like woodsmoke, and I imagined her sitting around a campfire cooking a hotdog on a stick. Her pant-legs were hooked with thistles, and I knew she'd been running through fields. Her boots left a trail of dried mud over the floor. For lunches, she ate salads of fireweed and dandelions. On sunny days, we sat together on the dock, watching the birds and fishing boats come and go. We didn't talk much. Bonnie seemed lost in her thoughts, caught up in the scenery. She was friendly enough, but she stayed a little apart from the rest. The other girls clowned together; Bonnie smiled to herself.

And then one morning Bonnie came to work without her pack. I remarked on its absence.

"I finally parked it," she said. "I found a cabin out the road." She described her landmarks—a hill, a red barn. I knew them; I lived past them. If she wanted a ride home, I told her, I was glad to give her a lift.

That evening we bumped out the road in my pickup. Bonnie talked about exploring old roads and cutoffs, how she'd found a log cabin that was practically overgrown. I didn't know the one she meant, but the old homesteads were littered with abandoned cabins. I'd lived in one myself at one point. It was back in the hills, a two-mile walk from any road—still standing, as far as I knew. I'd spent most of my time there developing the art of catching rainwater under holes in the roof; the pitch of the plinks in glass jars and coffee cans told me how full they were.

Bonnie pressed her face to the window, watching the bay and the mountains as we drove along the coast.

"What makes it blue?" she asked.

"What?"

"The ice. The glaciers. It's the most amazing color."

I took my eyes off the road long enough to look across the bay. We were even with the middle of the three glaciers that wound down from the mountains. The bottom of the glacier, where the snow had melted off, was a thick tongue of blue ice ridged with darker streaks of glacial moraine. It *was* an amazing color; I'd almost forgotten how amazing. Why were glaciers blue? I'd known at one time but no longer remembered the explanation. Something about the density, the way the light was absorbed or reflected. I said something to this effect, which seemed to satisfy Bonnie. She rolled down her window and let her hair stream out.

"Have you lived here your whole life?" she asked.

"Not yet," I joked. "Only since I was twenty."

"I'm twenty," she said. She twisted her hair into a knot. "You seem like you would have been born here."

I had to smile. I often wondered where I might have ended up if I'd been born in Alaska. If I'd started here, would I have found the life it offered so satisfying? Perhaps, like Jim, I'd have sought out other places. I wasn't even sure I'd ever have come back. But here I was, so much at home I could be mistaken for a born-and-bred.

I told Bonnie that I'd been brought up in Minnesota and that one spring, lured by adventure, a girlfriend and I hitchhiked up the

Al-Can Highway. My friend left at the end of the summer, but I stayed, first in that cabin with the leaky roof, later sharing a sprawling, drafty house near the beach with several new friends and friends of friends, an ever-changing collection of vegetarians and concertina players. Eventually I'd purchased an unfinished house in the woods. I'd hauled water, cut my own firewood, worked at odd jobs, added windows and insulation to my house. It all sounded so easy, telling it now. It hadn't been easy, but somehow it had seemed *necessary*. It was the way Alaskans lived. If, over time, I'd gradually quit my outhouse for an inside toilet and forfeited a portion of my firewood for an electric heater, that was also the Alaskan way.

Bonnie asked, "Didn't you ever get married?"

"No, I never did." I thought of Jim; my relationship with him was the closest I'd come, though it could hardly be called close when we'd never even talked about marriage. We'd once discussed living together, but neither of us wanted to move, and we'd each made faces at the idea of putting up with each other's moods on a regular basis.

But I didn't want to talk about myself. I didn't want to sound like I was bragging about how I'd made my own way in Alaska. It sounded too much like the old refrain we'd all heard as kids; our elders had always walked farther to school, in deeper snow, after having milked more cows.

"So," I asked, "do you think you'll be staying here?"

"In Alaska? Oh, yes. This is where I belong."

She said it with such conviction, I knew exactly what she meant. So many people, when they reach Alaska, no matter where they've started from, share that sense of finally coming home. In the early 1970s, a whole generation had seemed to feel that way. Most of us from that era were still around—pig-tailed men going bald on top, women in long skirts and insulated boots. Many of us had children— named Spruce and Willow and Sunrise—who were nearly grown now, nearly Bonnie's age. But I didn't think they were like Bonnie. I saw them at the high school, the boys wrestling or playing basketball, the girls applying eye makeup in the restroom. Maybe I wasn't so unusual in my time; maybe Bonnie was.

"And your parents?" I asked. "What do they think about you being here?"

Bonnie shrugged. "They weren't real excited when I told them I wanted to live off the land. They don't understand that, wanting to be one with Nature."

Ah, yes. Nature. My impulse was to sigh, a deep down-in-my-chest sigh for all the Being with Nature my peers and I had gone through, from dragging sleds through the mud to scraping moose hides. I wondered if Bonnie realized how recently the fields around us had been buried in snow. If Alaska wasn't quite the frozen waste-land that many people imagined, neither was it all that generous a land. I stifled my sigh. Bonnie would learn what the realities were. Meanwhile, let her chase her dreams. Young people think they can do anything. Maybe they can.

All I said was, "Summer's always too short."

Bonnie was eager to have me see her new home, so I parked at the turnout and walked into the woods with her, down a rutted road and then single-file across a field, along a winding trail that might have been made by horses. Bonnie led the way, carefully, as though she was trying to tread lightly, to flatten as few grasses as possible. Swallows skimmed past us, feeding on mosquitoes. Neither of us said anything. At the bottom of a slope, we entered another forested area. When I looked ahead I saw the roof setting an edge against the sky.

It wasn't much. The cabin was small, maybe ten by twelve, and low, with grass and the dead stalks of last year's cow parsnip over-growing the front, south-facing wall. Judging from the ill-fitting corner notches, the builder had been something less than a crafts-man. I guessed it had been an original homestead cabin, built in a hurry to provide some immediate shelter and satisfy a prove-up re-quirement. These "temporary" cabins had sprung up all over the country following World War II. Meant for one winter, many be-came the only homes families had for years. There was never quite enough money or time for the "real" house; all too often the man spent the building season elsewhere, working for wages. Maybe the family didn't last. Maybe the first winter was too much, and they went back to wherever they'd come from. In any case, forty years later, the country was spotted with these wrecks of abandoned cabins.

Bonnie drew my attention to the door handle. It was wood, cut from a spruce root and polished by handling to a smooth dirt-grained brown. It was nothing, really–nothing unusual for an old cabin built where what was at hand was cheaper and easier than what was not–but Bonnie was clearly taken with it. She closed her hand firmly around it and pushed the heavy door open. Like all cabin doors in Alaska, it opened inward, away from the banks of snow that pile up against it during winter storms.

Inside, I was struck by the smell–damp, like wet leaves and musty burlap, like the inside of some animal's den. The plywood floor, which slanted toward the door, sprang under my feet. It took a moment for my eyes to adjust. Light streamed in weakly through two small windows, one partially filled with cardboard, both streaked with dirt and cobwebs. The only color in the room was a bright purple sleeping bag unrolled on a platform, against one wall. Other than the platform, the only furnishings were a counter of sorts that ran under the broken window, a cable spool table, and two sections of log that served as stools. The remains of a sheet-metal stove shed huge flakes of rust; the stovepipe was gone, and rain had been coming in through the hole in the roof, falling onto the stove and floor.

I found the whole place immensely depressing.

"Home sweet home," Bonnie said. "Can I offer you some water? There's a *great* spring just out back."

I accepted a drink from her canteen. As I tipped my head back, I couldn't help wondering what had happened to whoever had built the cabin. Who were they? Where had they gone? What busted dreams had they taken with them, or left behind? And the others– the ones who'd come later, who'd laid down the strip of linoleum, who'd stuffed fiberglass insulation into the spaces between logs– what had become of *them?*

I handed back the canteen. The water tasted like the container, like plastic. It wasn't cold, and yet I felt like shivering. If I'd believed in ghosts, I would have sworn they were there with us. They were laughing, not with pleasure but with derision. No, they were frowning, commiserating. No, it was nothing, just a breeze blowing in the door behind us, just a mosquito whining. It was just me, remembering cold feet on colder cabin floors.

Bonnie settled herself onto one of the log stools. As she did, a vole streaked past her feet and disappeared under the bed platform.

I have little patience for voles, shrews, mice, or anything else that nests in my clothes and runs across me when I'm asleep in bed. "Looks like you need some mousetraps," I said.

Bonnie had leaned over and was peering after the vole. "No. I wouldn't do that. They were here first. I like them."

"They'll get into your food," I said.

"I don't care. I don't mind sharing."

"No, really," I said. I looked at what was laid out on the table: a camp stove, a squeeze tube of honey, a plastic bag of granola knotted at the top to keep it closed. "At least put things in jars. Like this," I said, lifting the bag. Granola spilled from a hole in one corner. "See, they've already gotten into this. I'll give you some jars." From behind the bag, four little turds, like black grains of rice, left a trail across the table.

Bonnie shrugged. "That's okay. I really don't mind."

"I have lots of jars. Look, they left some presents for you. You don't want to eat their shit, do you?"

"I don't want to have a lot of jars, either."

For some reason, I wouldn't let it go. Appreciation of nature could only go so far. I insisted, "One jar, then. I'll bring you *one* jar tomorrow."

Bonnie leaned over the table to look at the turds, then brushed them onto the floor. "I thought I left my mother a few thousand miles behind me," she said. "I can protect myself from mice. Honest." She looked up, but as soon as she caught my eye she looked away again. It was quiet in the cabin, without so much as the ticking of a clock. It was time for me to go. I mumbled something about how nice the long days were, and said good-bye.

As I walked back to my truck, I remembered very clearly: the more my parents had told me living in Alaska was difficult and dangerous, the more determined I'd been to do it. Deprivation, inconvenience—those concepts meant nothing to me. I'd *wanted* to do without running water, refrigerators, carpeting, to live as closely as I could to what was still simple and wild. Sure, I'd eventually gotten over it, but not because I'd let anyone make things easier for me.

Gotten over it? I'd outgrown it, I guessed. My satisfaction with falling-down homesteads and views of snowy mountains had worn itself out. I couldn't delight in leaky roofs and indoor wildlife anymore. In a way, I supposed I envied Bonnie that.

I tried, after that, not to offer Bonnie unsolicited advice. She seemed more restrained with me, too, less eager to volunteer her enthusiasms, more stoic in her stance beside the cannery's conveyor belts. I offered her rides to or from work, but she kept another schedule, hitching to town earlier, running off along the beach at the end of our shift.

And then, just a week after I visited her cabin, she quit the cannery. Her apron passed to the next in line, and Bonnie all but disappeared from my life. I saw her once as I left the cannery, way down on the beach, bending over something in the tideline. Another time, when Jim and I were driving past the reservoir, I saw her sitting on a fence with a burlap bag slung over her shoulder; I waved, but I don't think she recognized me in Jim's truck. Both times she was by herself, and I wondered if she wasn't too solitary, too alone in her adventures. Another time, driving again, I saw a girl with long red hair sailing a frisbee to a young man in shorts; I wasn't sure it was her, but I thought it was.

And then one morning, late in July, when the fireweed blazed in the fields, there she was, hitchhiking toward town with her big pack. My first thought was that she was moving out, leaving town, and I was disappointed. This wasn't her place after all. She'd used it up and was moving on, just another transient. I stopped, and she set her pack in the truckbed and got in beside me.

"I've missed you at work," I said, meaning it.

"Oh," she said. "Well, I didn't need to make very much money."

"Are you leaving?"

"Yes. Well, sort of. Remember, I said I wanted to go across the bay? That's where I'm going."

I immediately felt heartened. Bonnie wasn't letting me down after all. Across the bay, really, was better than out the road, for what she wanted. I was tempted to say something, to indicate my approval, but my approval wasn't what mattered. Still, I was curious. I asked her, "Where across the bay?"

"Just across. I thought I'd catch a ride with a fishing boat, and just go wherever it can drop me off."

"By yourself?"

"By myself."

My head filled with warnings. Don't fall off any cliffs. Don't break a leg. Look out for bears. Be careful. The voices—grave and tediously grumbled—belonged to my mother and father, when I was twenty, telling me I shouldn't be by myself in Alaska. I hadn't wanted or needed their warnings then; no harm had befallen me. I didn't need to repeat them now.

I only asked her how long she planned to be there.

"My goal is a year."

I had misunderstood, apparently. I had thought she was going *camping*. A few days, maybe a week or two. Had she arranged to stay in a cabin? No. She'd just told me she was headed, not for a particular place, but wherever a boat could drop her.

I glanced sideways and saw that she was staring straight ahead, determined.

"Bonnie, Bonnie, Bonnie," I said.

"What?"

"Winter is something else over there. Even fall, even a couple weeks from now. It rains like you wouldn't believe."

"It's something I want to do," she said. "I just want to live there and see what happens. Be a part of Nature."

Good old Nature again. Life at its essence. I stopped myself from saying anything. It was still summer, and rain had never melted anyone yet. Bonnie could always change her goal as soon as she had enough scenery and sand, as soon as the weather turned ugly. She'd learn something for sure, and be the better for it.

"Well," I said, "I hope you have plenty of matches."

I took her all the way to the boat ramp. Along the way, I talked about people at work, about Etta's swollen legs and a new girl who'd lasted less than an hour. I told her that if she wanted to come back to the cannery again, I could probably get her on. We'd be doing salmon into September, and then halibut, and then crab. I told her I was looking forward to having the winter off; maybe I'd even go to Hawaii in January.

Then, when she was getting her pack from the back, I leaned out
the window and said, "Keep in touch." I realized right away that that
didn't make any sense. A picture flashed in my mind of her sticking a
message in a bottle and tossing it into the bay. What I really wanted
to let her know was that she was welcome back anytime.

She thanked me for the ride. The last I saw of her was her red hair
flaring out around her pack as she strode off toward the ramp. She
looked so purposeful, bearing down on the boats in her oversized
black cannery boots.

It wouldn't have surprised me to have seen Bonnie back in town
before the summer was out. The blackflies would have been too
much for her, or she'd have gotten lonely at last. Or food—she'd at
least have needed to come in to buy beans and rice.

But if she came to town, I didn't see her. Of course, there wasn't
any reason why I would have. She wouldn't have been likely to look
me up. Seeing her would have had to be luck; I'd have had to run into
her at the grocery store or spot her beside the road, waiting for a ride.

And I was busy. I was still working at the cannery and in my garden. In August, three of my cousins, people I hadn't seen in twenty-
odd years, drove into town in a Winnebago, and I showed them the
hot fishing holes and scenic vistas. As soon as they left, I made a trip
to Fairbanks to see a friend and the Indian-Eskimo Olympics. Jim
was in and out, always carrying a broken pump or some other boat
part he needed me to find a replacement for.

Whenever Bonnie drifted into my thoughts it was with a sort of
tidal action that would wash in and wash out, tossing one more piece
of flotsam into my already-littered mind. Life on the other side, with
all its tranquility, finally seemed not such a bad idea. When I pictured Bonnie making campfires on the beach, watching the birds, I
almost wanted to change places.

And then summer began to get behind us. The sun went down
earlier, returning us to nights that were dark, pinpricked with stars.
Mornings, the grass around my house was bent with the weight of a
silvery dew. The fireweed blossoms closed up into dull purple
sheaths, and then the sheaths burst open, releasing the seeds on
wind-blown fluff that swept past the windows like snow. Bonnie, if

she was still on the other side, would have been even more aware of the changes.

The fall rains began, cold rains, the kind that comes in solid sheets, blown sideways by the wind. I stood in my house with the heat of the woodstove on my backside and looked out through the blur at the leaden sky. Jim was butchering crab in my kitchen, nearly lost in the steam that billowed from my huge cauldron. I was glad he was with me; it was the sort of weather that makes me want company. I thought out loud.

"She couldn't still be there."

"Who?"

"Bonnie. That red-haired girl from the cannery. Remember? We saw her that day by the reservoir. You haven't seen her recently, have you?"

"I've only heard you fussing about her." He slid a five-gallon bucket across the floor.

"I don't fuss," I said. "I only wish I'd asked her to let me know when she came back, so I could stop wondering."

Jim made a point of peering out a steamy window. "Oh, she's *back*," he said. "Where did she live, anyway?"

"She was staying in that old cabin. Remember, I told you it was a grungy, depressing place."

"But where was she *from*? New York, wasn't it?"

"Upstate New York. I don't even remember the name of the town."

"So there."

"There what?"

"She's gone back home."

I wasn't so sure. I knew that once *I'd* come to Alaska, I resented anyone suggesting that home was anywhere *but* Alaska. I didn't know if Bonnie felt the same way, but she'd certainly never made any sounds about going back to New York. But then, if she came back from the other side, I didn't know what reasons she'd have to stay in the area. Certainly the old cabin, even if she'd fixed it up, couldn't be that attractive. She might have gone anywhere.

"Here's one for you," Jim said. "Why does the ocean roar?"

I couldn't guess.

"Because it's got crabs on its bottom."

I knew Jim was trying to cheer me up, so I managed a smile. He had to be right. By the time the rains started, Bonnie had sneaked back to town and headed out, perhaps all the way back to New York. I boosted myself up to sit on the counter. "It's funny," I said. "I go back and forth between wanting to *be* her and wanting to take care of her."

Jim put his hands on my knees. "Sarah, you are not her mother."

"That's what she said."

He turned back to his crab and started to sing. *My Bonnie lies over the ocean, my Bonnie lies over the sea*. He couldn't remember the next line, and neither could I. He hummed his way to *Bring back my Bonnie to me*, then sang the chorus like a sailor, one arm in front and one in back, hopping from leg to leg. I couldn't help but laugh.

Jim was the one to call me in November.

"Have you seen this week's paper? There's an ad."

I didn't like the tone of his voice. I knew right away it wasn't an ad for a boat or radio or anything he wanted either of us to buy.

"What?"

He read it. "Information requested concerning the whereabouts of Bonnie Erickson. Call the Alaska Troopers."

He didn't say anything else, as though he was waiting for me.

"What else does it say?"

"That's it. A picture and a description. Red hair. The troopers' number. Was that her last name?"

"Yes."

"Are you going to call?"

"Of course."

We hung up, but I didn't call the troopers right away. I stood by the window, looking out into the night. That morning, I'd noticed the snowline on the mountains across the bay had dropped almost to eye level. Now, nothing except blackness lay in that direction. All I could see in the window was the inside of my house reflected – the bright lights, the pink and green afghan on the couch, a thin woman with a long, dark face and rounded shoulders. I placed one hand against the window. The glass was cold.

I went over all the possibilities. She could have drowned. She could have poisoned herself with baneberries or paralytic clams. She could have fallen off a cliff or, if she managed to climb up onto a glacier, into a crevasse, or a tree could have fallen on her. A bear could have attacked her. She could have gotten too wet and cold and succumbed to hypothermia. She could even have been victimized by some sick or evil person; she could have been murdered and dropped to the bottom of the bay in a crab pot.

On the other hand, she could be perfectly all right. She could have moved into a cabin, and be warm and dry. She could even have met someone—one of those bushy men who would be glad for a help-mate. She could have come back a long time ago; she could be in town, or some other town or state, or anywhere. For all I knew, perhaps she never even went across the bay; what if, instead, she'd taken a job on a fishing boat and was trawling in the Bering Sea?

Outside, the wind rattled bare branches and whistled in the eaves. I did know one thing. She couldn't still be camping, under nylon and clouds, with the snowline descending on her.

Finally, I called the troopers. I was the first person to answer the ad. Her parents, in New York, had reported her missing. They hadn't heard from her since July, and they'd begun to worry.

I wasn't much help. All I could tell them was that I knew Bonnie from the cannery, that I'd given her a ride on a day late in July, and that she'd told me she was going wherever she could find a boat ride to and hoped to stay a year.

The trooper sounded incredulous. "A year?"

"That was her *goal*. I didn't really think she would." I felt the silence on the other end as disapproval. "I mean," I said, "how could she, unless she moved into a cabin and did a whole lot more planning and provisioning? I think she's quite resourceful," I added. "She's very independent."

The trooper took my number and promised to let me know if they got more information.

I called Jim back.

"I want to go look at that cabin where Bonnie was staying. Will you go with me?"

"When?"

"Right now. I have this feeling that she might have left something there, or there might be some sign of her coming back. Or maybe someone else is living there now—someone who might know something."

I knew that the last thing in the world Jim wanted to do at nine o'clock on a cold, windy, November night was to drive out from town and tramp through the dark to look at an old cabin. I also knew that he'd do it. Twenty minutes later, he was banging on my door, flashlight in hand.

We drove back to the turnout, then hiked the trail. The wind had come up stronger. The big spruce were swaying and creaking; dead alder leaves blew into us like attacking bats. Jim and I aimed our flashlights ahead, but neither of us said anything.

No light shone from the cabin. In the dark and without its surround of grass, it looked particularly bleak and forlorn, a rotting shell. I opened the door.

"She lived *here*? Jim tested the floor, feeling the plywood give under his feet.

I didn't answer. My flashlight beam cut back and forth across the cabin. The bed platform, the table, the stump stools. The broken window, the stove, the flakes of rust, the dirt. Except for the absence of Bonnie's few possessions, the cabin was the same as I'd seen it when she'd first moved in. She'd never cleaned it up, never tried to make any repairs or improvements, never made it her own.

Jim was shining his light on the table. There wasn't much there: a cardboard pepper shaker, a broken bootlace, and a primitive sort of cup made from birchbark. I picked up the cup to examine it. Someone had started with a strip of brittle bark, then tried to fold it into a funnel shape. The bottom and side were sewn together with what looked like root, but the holes were too large, and the root was broken off and retied into clumsy, thick knots at various points. Dried blossoms of pink clover filled the bottom of the cup.

I held it out for Jim to look at.

He looked unimpressed. "Is that hers?"

"I suppose so. I suppose she made it." I sniffed at the clover, but there wasn't any smell. I set the cup back on the table.

We went over the rest of the cabin, shining our lights into every corner, over every skeletal leaf. I didn't really know what I was hoping for. Some sort of "clue," I supposed—a piece of map, a scrap of paper with something written on it, anything that might suggest more than what I already knew. Finally we ended up back at the table. Jim balanced his flashlight on end so that it pointed upright, illuminating the dark roof boards in a dull circle. I snapped mine off. I wanted Jim to tell me not to worry. I wanted him to remind me that I wasn't her mother. He didn't. He was waiting for me. I wondered if the cup meant anything. Had Bonnie been practicing for life in the wilderness? And the clover? What good was clover? I turned my light back on.

"Let's get out of here," I said.

We went home, and I waited, over the next days and weeks. One weekend the local rescue squad crossed the bay and scouted along the coast, but they didn't find anything.

Winter closed in quickly. It snowed often and hard; snow covered fence posts and buried parked cars. I replayed in my mind every conversation I'd ever had with Bonnie as I tried to figure out where she might have gone, what she'd wanted to do. I went to sleep with the picture in my mind of her striding off in her cannery boots; I awoke in the night thinking I heard her footsteps on my porch, only slowly coming to recognize the thuds as snow falling from the roof.

And then, at last, it was spring again. The snow melted. The roads turned to mud and potholes. I could smell the ocean again, and the earth as it warmed. Green shoots erupted on the south-facing slopes; I planted my garden. And then it was summer, and the sun was high. Salmon ran the beaches, work at the cannery was fast-paced, the fireweed bloomed. Jim was fishing, filling his boat hold repeatedly, having his best season ever. People at the cannery mentioned the red-haired girl; they remembered her as a good worker, but distant. Everyone spoke of her in the past tense.

Yesterday, clam diggers in Tuskatan Cove went ashore to climb over rocks and eat lunch. Back in the brush, atop a knoll, children found shreds of a purple sleeping bag, scattered belongings, Bonnie's bones.

And so, I am on the beach, walking, by myself. The tide is out, the bay choppy. Fall is in the air: a subtle chill, a softer light, a taste in my mouth like regret. I'm reminded of practical duties; it's nearing time to haul more wood, caulk around windows, order new felt liners for my winter boots.

No one knows how Bonnie died. Pathologists will test her bones for poisons and malnutrition. Other causes of death are harder to confirm. We only know that she was never far from help. There were cabins on both sides of the cove, a mile in either direction; from anywhere on the beach she might have signaled a passing boat or plane.

Jim heard the news on the fishing grounds. He called me through the marine operator. The shore-based end of marine calls can be picked up on any boat, so I'm always careful about what I say. I just said that I had heard, too, and that, yes, I was sad, but I was okay. I was okay. After all, it wasn't really unexpected, her being found not alive.

Jim said he was sorry. He meant, for me, because I was sad, because I had known Bonnie and had worried about her. "She must have been crazy," he said. "She must have wanted to die." I suppose he was trying to make me feel better.

I know differently, though. She wasn't crazy, and she didn't want to die. A crazy or suicidal person wouldn't have been enchanted with the flapping of gulls or seen the shine in a wooden door handle. But not to die—not to die in this place—takes other skills, adjustments, compromises. We live our lives, from one cup of coffee and seasonal job to the next, in narrowing circles, limiting the risks. We pad our lives with comforts; we limit the chances we take with our surroundings, with our relationships, with ourselves.

Somehow, over the years, the part of me that had been so ready for adventure, so accepting of hardship, so enthralled with what was new and simple and natural had become less ready, less accepting, less enthralled. It hadn't been anything specific, any *event* that had changed me. It had just happened, a process, the same sort of dimming adjustment my eyes had made to the glaciers' blue ice after I'd seen it enough times.

I'm saddened by Bonnie's death, not because, in the face of her determination, I could have prevented it, but because in my life, when I might have sought more, I settled, increasingly, for what was safer, and less.

Down the beach an arctic tern flutters in midair, inspecting something in the surf, and then soars away, out over the bay. I stand and watch as it shrinks smaller, as it fades into the pale sky. I watch until it disappears, and then I continue to watch the spot where it disappeared.

The Winner

Mitchell sat at his window, eating a bowl of soup and watching a cow moose and two yearlings work their way across the slope. They munched through the willows that ran along a boggy area and then picked at some green shoots coming up through the grass. They were so close that Mitchell could see a couple of dark lumps—what he took for the budding of antlers—on the larger yearling's head. Then the cow stopped chewing and looked up. Mitchell could hear someone singing. *If I were a rich man, yabadabadabadabadabadabadoo.* A minute later, when the three moose had moved off to the side, Lew beat on the door.

"What's happening?" Lew asked, sitting down in the only chair.

"Not much," Mitchell answered. "Having some dinner." Whatever meal Mitchell ate, regardless of the time of day, he called "dinner."

Lew lifted himself to try to see what Mitchell was eating. "More cat stew?"

"Give me a break," Mitchell said, more from habit than from any hope that Lew would. He'd tired long ago of explaining that a person can take only so much from a cat. Every time Mitchell opened the door, his tom used to dash in and spray the wall. The whole house smelled like cat piss, and he got to where he couldn't stand it any longer. He wasn't cruel about it. Other people would have beat the cat or dropped it off on some lonely road to starve. Mitchell had been very logical and humane; he'd held it on the splitting block and used the ax – one quick stroke.

It was after that he decided it really wasn't any different than a chicken or a rabbit, so he skinned it out and made a stew.

Mitchell was that kind of guy. "Waste not, want not," was his creed, and everything he did was frugal and efficient. He never bought anything he didn't need, and he never threw anything away. His sneakers were bound together with duct tape; he washed his hair with bar soap instead of spending money on shampoo. If cheese grew mold or lettuce slimed, he'd still choke it down. It was perfectly logical that he wouldn't waste good meat just because it belonged to a cat.

"So, what brings you by?" Mitchell asked.

Lew smiled. "Actually, I had a phone message for you. I thought I'd deliver it personal."

Lew was Mitchell's only friend who had a phone, and it was that number he gave, sparingly, as a message phone when he needed one. Quickly, he ran through the possibilities. There was always his mother, getting on in years back in Ohio. They rarely kept in touch, but she had the number, just in case. But Lew wasn't likely to be smiling if she'd just croaked. It could be he'd given it on some job application, though he wasn't really looking for work.

"I'm sorry to bother you," Mitchell said. "You didn't need to come tell me, probably, but I appreciate it."

"I thought you'd want to know right away," Lew said, his smile stretching tight over big front teeth.

"Well, it must be good news," Mitchell said flatly. "Why don't you spit it out?"

"I'll give you a hint," Lew said. He waited while Mitchell leaned into the window to look at the moose again. "The ice went out at Nenana."

Mitchell spun around. "The Ice Classic. I had a ticket." He clutched at his shirt as if feeling the pockets for his ticket. "What day is it?"

Lew slowly reached into his pants pocket and pulled out a folded slip of paper. He unfolded it, even more slowly, and read, "May ninth, 1:11 P.M. Nine winners. Twenty thousand, one hundred fifty-two dollars each." His smile broke over his big teeth.

Every year the city of Nenana sold $2 tickets all over Alaska for guesses at the day and minute the Tanana River ice would break up, toppling a tripod. The winners—there were always several—shared the pot. Mitchell had never bought a ticket, but this year, walking into town, he'd found a blank ticket lying on the road. Not to be wasteful, he'd filled in a guess and delivered it to one of the collection boxes.

Now, Mitchell stood with his hands spread over his front pockets as though he were doing a double flag salute. "They called you?" he said.

"Yeah. You know, you put a phone number on the ticket, and then they call the winners. The lady said the checks would go out right away. Certified." He looked at the slip of paper in his hand again. "1:11 P.M. Now how'd you know that?"

Mitchell dropped his hands to his sides. He didn't remember what date and time he'd picked. It had just been a guess, based on something he didn't remember anymore—maybe the time on the clock at the liquor store when he filled it out or something about the number one that was in his head that day. But Lew—Lew wasn't above pulling his leg. Hadn't he told him just last week that the barmaid at The Palace had asked about him, and then when they went in to have a few—that Mitchell paid for—she didn't even look at him? Mitchell narrowed his eyes. "How do I know it's true?"

"Shit, man," Lew said, falling back in the chair. "Would I kid about something like this? Honest, it was this lady with a kind of shrill voice—reminded me of my sister. She was very excited for you. In fact"—he tossed the slip of paper onto the floor so that Mitchell had to stoop to pick it up—"she left their phone number in case you wanted to call back and tell them how glad you are. Not on my nickel, though. Go find a pay phone."

Lew rocked back and forth in the chair that was not a rocker but an armchair with broken, uneven legs. Mitchell studied the paper, tracing the shape of the numbers and letters, made with a pen that was a bit stop-and-go with the ink supply. The way they were scribbled—it looked like something Lew would have copied down from the phone, not something he would have planned out. $20,152. That was a lot of money to have fall into your hands.

"Supposing it's true," Lew said, "and that I'm not a bastard after all—which I am not—don't you think it's worth some celebrating? You got some of that home brew you could break loose of?"

$20,152. Mitchell looked at it one more time and then stuck the paper into his shirt pocket, snapping the flap shut over it. "I'll get you, I really will, if this is a setup." He walked into the back room and pulled a couple of bottles from a box beneath the bed.

Lew called in after him. "If it's not the truth, you can eat my dog, Mitchell. I swear on it."

Mitchell opened the bottles and leaned against the counter as he drank. Lew finished his first and hefted himself from the chair, saying, "Can I get you another?" as he hobbled into the back room.

"Thanks, no," Mitchell said, pulling from his pocket a bandless digital watch—another springtime find, a little rusted along the sides but still working, only an hour off. He hadn't figured out yet how to bring it up to daylight savings time. It was already after four o'clock. He didn't want to lose any more time getting down the hill to a telephone. If it wasn't true, Lew wouldn't stick around long. If it was, well, then he wouldn't grudge him another beer or two. Mitchell finished his and banged the bottle down on the counter. He took his jacket from the nail behind the door and his pack from the corner. "Well, I guess I'll go see if I'm famous yet," he said. "I got groceries to get anyway."

Mitchell wove his way down through the field and into the trees, through the last traces of snow. Lower down, the bluff fell off sharply, and he followed the trail over a hogback between ravines. Piles of moose droppings littered the way, flattening like malt balls underfoot, and in low spots the trail was slick with mud. Below, the roofs of town lay like dark squares among the scattered spruce. The sounds of kids playing, cars bucking over the washboarded roads, and dogs barking carried up the hill. The same air currents supported an eagle's cruise along the bluff; Mitchell watched it circle and then glide off above. It was so weird, that he could feel really *out there*, when this whole crowded town lay just over the edge. No one ever came by his place, except for an occasional skier or snowmachiner in winter, and yet the town lay only ten minutes beneath his feet. People stuck to roads—the ones below and the ones that wound up the bluff east and west of him and connected atop the ridge, a mile above his cabin.

Every time he thought of the money he pushed it back out of his mind. It didn't do to speculate until he knew if it was true. $20,152!

In the phone booth by the theater Mitchell laid out his change and placed the call. A man answered, and in the background Mitchell could hear a party.

"I got a message," Mitchell said, "that I've got a winning ticket. I'd like to find out if it's true."

"Well, what's your name?" the man shouted. "I can't tell you unless I know your name. Ha! Ha! Ha!"

Mitchell saw how easily he could be trapped. The guy was drunk. Any name he gave, he'd probably laugh and say it was a winner. "Burt Eastwood," he said, pulling the name combination off the movie marquee.

"Is that in a pool?" the man asked, suddenly sober.

"No," Mitchell said, embarrassed. "How 'bout Edward Mitchell? Not in a pool. Just one guy."

"You're on!" the man yelled, and he read Mitchell's address to him. "The checks are already written! They go out in the morning!"

Mitchell hung up. It was a fact.

Outside the booth, Mitchell looked up and down the street to see if there was anyone he knew driving or walking by. A fat motorhome plastered with stickers lumbered one way, and a low, mufflerless Chevy whizzed by the other in an explosion of dust and loud music. Mitchell shouldered his pack and walked off toward the health food store.

There, he picked through the crate marked *Smoothie Fruit*. It was everything that was overripe, bruised, or damaged—cheap and okay for blending up in a drink or otherwise making the best of. He chose a melon and some single brown bananas. Shit, man, he thought. Tomorrow I'll be famous, and the next day I'll be rich. I can go a little extra. He selected a bunch of young asparagus for $1.89 a pound and didn't even weigh it out. Then he went around to the other end of the store and found a can of real maple syrup. He came back to the bins of nuts and shoveled out three scoops of pistachios. Then, in the cooler, he picked out not the jack cheese that was on special but a nice block of Jarlsberg. He hadn't *ever* bought the imported cheeses, or pistachios, or real Vermont maple syrup, not in his life.

The beautiful woman with the long, shiny brown hair was work-ing at the checkout counter. Mitchell lined up his purchases in front of her. She began to ring them up, pushing them past, her face set in straight-forward concentration, as though they were all normal items. Mitchell watched her but she never even looked up at him. He knew her name was Kim, and he was pretty sure she knew his. He was in the store often enough, buying his food and signing the array of petitions that were always laid out on the counter—for the nuclear freeze, for moose habitat, against cutting trees.

"I don't suppose you've heard," he said.

She looked up then, just for a split second between the cheese and the asparagus. "What?"

"I won the Ice Classic." It sounded odd to him, coming so calmly from his lips.

She glanced up again. "How nice," she said. "Congratulations." She hit the total button and the register rang and kicked out its drawer. "Twenty-nine forty," she said.

Mitchell took his wad of money from his pocket and laid out three tens. "Keep the change," he said, stuffing the groceries into his pack. He saw her put the bills into the drawer, hesitate, then bang the drawer shut. She walked away from behind the counter and began restocking the vitamin shelves.

Some people just don't know how to deal with wealth and fame, Mitchell thought. He elbowed into his pack and wiggled until the load felt comfortable enough.

Walking back along the main street, it occurred to Mitchell that he could afford to get a new backpack to replace the army one he'd trucked around with for the last nineteen years. It was getting pretty grubby, finally, and most of the ties were broken off. Jesus, he thought. If it was a kid, it would be grown up. He stopped at the sports shop in the center of town.

"I'd like to see what you've got in packs," he said to the young man, "like this one here." He turned to indicate the one he wore.

"Well," the young man said, "we don't carry Army-Navy. But I can show you what we have." He led Mitchell to a wall display. "You probably want something like this," he said, placing his hand on a bright blue sack with all kinds of pockets and nylon straps hanging off it. "It's got an internal fiberglass frame and a suspension system that allows you to adjust the weight on your hips." He flipped the pack over and pulled on one of the straps. "This here hitches it in toward your back, so the weight doesn't pull on your shoulders. And this cordura," he said, stroking the fabric, "is both durable and waterproof. And this"—he pulled a nylon sleeve out of the top of the pack—"is a bivie sack."

Mitchell looked at him blankly. "A bivie sack? Pray tell."

"Bivouac. You know, if you get caught out, or if you want to travel light anyway, you can just put your legs in the pack and pull the bivie sack up around the rest of you. And, of course, it's got all nylon zippers."

Mitchell reached out and touched the pack. "I s'pose it's got a special place to carry eggs."

"Eggs?"

"Chicken eggs. Like home from the store."

The young man turned to a shelf opposite. "We do actually." He picked up a couple of plastic boxes, molded into egg-shapes. "Two sizes—either four or six. For a dozen eggs, you'd need two sixes. Or, I suppose, three fours. They're generally used for backpacking—so you can have fresh eggs on the trail."

"Well, I'm just looking today," Mitchell said, anxious to escape. "I'll think on it."

"Of course we also have the external frame packs," the young man said.

Mitchell walked quickly to the corner and cut through the parking lot at the grocery store. By the store entrance, a couple of kids were sitting with a large cardboard box. Mitchell stopped to see what they had.

Each of the boys held a kitten in his lap, and two more were curled up in the box. "Wanna kitten?" one of the boys asked.

Mitchell remembered his old tom, not without some fondness. It was nice to have company, sometimes. He just couldn't abide that one's particular habits. "Cute little guys, aren't they?" he said, reaching down to stroke the gray one the boy held.

"You want this one?" the kid said. "You can have it."

"No," Mitchell said. "I haven't had such good luck with cats."

"His mom's gonna take them to the pound," the other boy said. "Then they'll kill them."

"Oh, they don't kill them," Mitchell said. "They find new homes for them. Didn't you ever hear of anyone going to the pound to get a new pet? Why, that's what people do all the time."

"They got too many already," the first boy said.

Mitchell caressed the soft fur, and the kitten rumbled into a purr. It stared up at him with big blue eyes; it looked like one of those pictures they always had in dentists' offices—of big-eyed animals and children. Actually, he thought, the reason his tom was such a problem was that he had all his male parts. Now he could afford to get a cat fixed.

"You guys gonna sell used cars when you grow up? Or plastic egg cartons? You just talked me into it."

"How many?" the first boy asked.

"How many! What are you guys trying to do to me?"

"They like to play together," the second boy said. "It's good to have more than one."

Mitchell leaned over into the box. Hell, the vet would probably give him a discount on two fixes. "Why don't you give me that there striped one and the gray one. That way I can tell them apart."

Both boys leapt up, shoving the kittens into his hands. "All *right!*" The first one gave the gray one a final pat on the head. "You be good," he said.

It was awkward hiking up the road and then the trail with a kitten in each hand, clutched against the front of his jacket. Mitchell was used to swinging his arms as he strode. He didn't want to put the kittens in his pack, though—not with all that good food. His hands grew wet from the heat of their little, pulsing bodies, and their fur matted with the moisture.

Alone at last, away from the bustle and distraction of town, Mitchell began to think about the money. $20,152 was a lot of dough. He didn't think he'd really get a new pack; his old one had life left in it yet. He'd get the cats fixed when they got old enough. He'd probably get roped into buying a round of drinks. May as well count that, and just hope it wasn't too crowded when Lew and the others dragged him in. What else? He supposed he could get his teeth fixed, but the way he felt about that was that it didn't make sense to have your teeth outlast you. There were a lot of people getting buried these days with a fortune worth of perfect teeth. The rest of you wore out, so why shouldn't your teeth too?

Most people, they'd probably buy a new car and take a vacation. But Mitchell didn't want a car. When he owned a truck, it was just one broken part after another. It was easier to borrow one off a buddy if he needed to haul in a load of coal. And hell, vacation? His whole life was a vacation. On the homestead all he had to do for the owners was clip down the raspberry bushes in the fall and be there so no one else would come around to mess up the land. Setting there with the moose and the birds, there wasn't anywhere else he wanted to go.

The kittens were getting all sweated up, so he stopped to rest and let them climb over his chest while he lay back against his pack. Birds flocked through the woods, chittering away. The town below was miniaturizing into lines and squares again.

On the other hand, the money was certainly his—won fair and square. Everyone else had the same chance. He might need it some-day. Waste not, want not.

When Mitchell got back to his cabin, Lew was asleep in his chair, the radio squawking news in the background. Mitchell snapped it off. Lew knew how to make himself at home, all right. He'd even cleared off the top of a wooden crate Mitchell used as a table and moved it over by the chair for a footstool. Without waking him, Mitchell put his groceries away. He counted empty beer bottles—the one he drank, three for Lew. The kittens meowed at the door.

Mitchell opened the door and sat sideways in it, his back against the jamb. The kittens piled into his lap. The sun had sunk into the trees; it blinked through the line of spruce as Mitchell moved his head back and forth. The hillside had taken on a greenish sheen in the angled light, as though the sun were reaching under the old dead mat to bring out the new growth. The smell—the day's warmth radi-ating back out of the earth—reminded Mitchell of towels dried on a clothesline.

He plucked a piece of dried grass from beside the step and tapped the kittens with it. They both batted at it. He drew the stem back and forth over the step and the kittens chased it, tumbling over themselves. The gray one nosedived off the end of the step, landing

with a grunt on the packed earth two feet below. It looked so surprised that Mitchell laughed.

Lew, stretching, got up from the chair. "You're back," he said. "I
must've dozed off." He stumbled toward the door and stopped with
one hand braced on the counter. "What the *hell*? What are you doing
with *cats*?" At the sound of his voice, both kittens scampered off
around the side of the cabin.

"Kittens," Mitchell said. "Meet my new kittens."

"What's the idea?" Lew pushed hair back out of his eyes. "You
gonna raise them up before you slaughter them?"

The striped kitten stuck its head around the corner, and Mitchell
shook the piece of grass, tempting it. "These ones, they're going to
get fixed so they don't have any bad habits. You know I've always
liked having animals around."

Lew hunkered down. "Here, kitty, kitty."

"They're shy," Mitchell said. He stared off down the hill.

"Well," Lew said. "I didn't feed you no line, did I? How's it feel?"
He leaned over and snapped his finger against Mitchell's knee.
"When are we gonna celebrate?"

"I s'pose you want me to buy you a beer downtown," Mitchell
said.

"Well, of course! A round for the house, and then some. That's
just what's done, man, in a case like this. You know, share the wealth
with your friends, and let some of your luck rub off."

Mitchell calculated. Three home brews today, an Oly at The
Palace the other day, less, say–being generous–a couple of home
brews for taking the call and bringing him the message. Of course,
then Lew was sitting in his chair, rearranging his furniture, and
wearing out his radio batteries. That ought to count for something.
He was still way ahead of him. Lew ought to be buying *him* a drink.

"Your check will be here probably the day after tomorrow, don't
you think?" Lew scratched his face. "Thursday. You wanna set a
time?"

Mitchell wondered what $20,152 would look like in bills. If he
cashed it all at once, how would they give it to him? He doubted the
dinky little bank in town had that kind of money–real money–on
hand. They'd probably have to bring in an armored car. He didn't
want to leave his money in the bank; besides losing control of their

computers all the time, they were going belly-up all over the country, taking people's savings with them. But then, he didn't really
want it all at once. That was too much money to carry, and muggers
might lie in wait for him along the trail home. They might do that
anyway, he realized, if they thought he had even a few hundred
bucks. Christ!

Lew was running his tongue around his mouth and over his teeth
as though sleeping had left him tasting a lot of dry cotton. "I bet you
still can't hardly believe it. I can't. What are you gonna do with that
much money? You must've been thinking about it."

He'd just have to be careful. Maybe make himself a little thing to
wear in his shoe so he could withdraw money from the bank, go in a
restroom, put it in his shoe, then walk home. He could take to carrying a walking stick—a real hefty one, with a pointed end. Little by
little he could get the money home and put it away in glass jars under
a floorboard.

"Mitchell!" Lew said. "You're not talking. You so excited you
don't know what to say? What's that expression—cat got your
tongue? Hah!"

Both kittens were back up on the step, chasing the piece of grass as
Mitchell swept it back and forth. Mitchell picked them up and
swung his legs around so that Lew could get out the door. "Well,
Lew, I sure thank you for bringing me the message. Even though I
bought at The Palace last week, and even though you just drank
three of my very best home brew—priceless stuff—yeah, I'll buy you
a beer on Thursday. Make it early. Three o'clock. Jack's."

"You cheap weasel," Lew said. "Right in the middle of a working
guy's day. And Jack's—there's no one that drinks there in the day-
time. You can't hardly fit ten people at the bar." He stepped out into
the yard and threw a hard look back at the kittens. The striped one
drew up its shoulders and sunk its claws into Mitchell's leg.

Mitchell watched Lew huff off up the hill. Some people, he
thought. They just can't deal with it. They don't know how to be
glad for you—they have to be jealous. They're not happy if they can't
rip you off.

In the cabin, Mitchell took his bag of pistachios from the drawer
and measured a third into a tin. The kittens scampered about under
his feet. "You guys must be hungry," he said. He mixed powdered

milk with water and set a small bowl on the floor for them. Under the floor—that was kind of an obvious place to keep money, but he could fix it so it was well hidden. He walked back and forth a few times, testing where the planks gave under his weight. Then he stopped and watched the kittens.

Drawn up on their haunches to drink, they looked like a pair of cheerleader pom-poms; their lapping sounded like a very polite applause. Mitchell clicked his heels together and bowed. Thank you very much, he said inside his head. The winner is—he waited a moment, savoring the appreciation—yes indeed, yours truly, Mr. Mitchell.

Marks

After wintering in the small Alaskan town she's begun to think of as home, Pam is back at the hatchery to mark salmon fry. On her breaks she walks along the creek, listening to its flow and breathing the scent of sun-warmed earth. Every day planes and helicopters fly overhead. Some of them, she knows, are part of the search effort. Evenings, listening to the radio news in the hatchery's common room, she hears the reports—another body discovered, another identified.

There are so many; it went on for so long, and no one noticed. No one missed them enough. Only when the last victim escaped, late in the fall, did anyone suspect what had been happening. That woman's story sticks in Pam's head, like the constant crash of water through the hatchery, chilling her anew each time it pushes through to the front of her consciousness. She sees it, as it must have happened again and again: The airplane landing on a remote sandbar; the man raping his victim and then freeing her to run; the man loading his gun, lacing his boots, preparing to hunt her down. The survivor somehow eluded him, plunging naked through the brush until, bloodied and hypothermic, she came upon a pair of fishermen two days later.

Investigators found an x'd map in the plane. Daily now, the troopers fly out along the river to the indicated spots. As winter retreats, the shallow graves, one by one, appear. Pam pictures them emerging from the sand and willow thickets like rugged wildflowers bursting through the last scraps of snow.

Pam slides now along the hatchery path, watching the mud pile up around the toes of her rubber boots; the layer of mud where the snow has melted off is slick over the frozen ground. Leaving the path, she crunches across snow patches to stand at the edge of the creek. She shoves her hands deep into the pockets of her down vest to warm them as she listens to the fine tinkling of water over rocks. It has a pitch to it, almost as high as that of shell ice washing away. The sound is one that, even if she were hearing it for the first time, she knows she would recognize as cold.

Stretching from side to side to ease the stiffness in her back, she moves off down the creek. Where it makes a jog, she stops above a pool. Shading her eyes against the glare, she watches for movement. The Dolly Varden should be in the creek now—in from the sea in search of salmon fry—but she doesn't see any.

When her ten minutes are up, Pam hurries back to the hatchery. It's so much colder inside, away from the sun. The creek water, passing through the building, spills down from the overhead pipes into the incubators and then along the concrete raceways. For the hatchery crew, working amidst the rush of water is like living under the constant cooling of the mists at the base of a waterfall.

The fin-marking "room" is in the middle, on a concrete slab between rows of incubators. A space heater glows inside the makeshift plastic tent. Pam slips through the opening and takes her seat next to the two other women. Between the slam of water and the belting out of a Linda Ronstadt song from the tape player, there's no chance of talk.

Pam dips a netful of salmon fry and dumps them into the basin on the table before her. The inch-long fish yield quickly to the anesthetic, flopping sideways so that they look like slivers of silver jewelry. They remind Pam of a necklace she saw once, elongated pieces strung together from their points, each element a slightly different shape, size, or curve.

It's amazing, really, how different each fry is from the next. Before beginning the marking program, Pam thought that a fry was a fry was a fry. How different, after all, could something like a baby fish be from any other of the same species? As it turns out, they're remarkably individualistic—one with a large head and a small body, another with a body thin behind the gills and widening below, one with large fins and another with small. Occasionally she finds a deformed one—hunched up or twisted like a corkscrew. *Just wait*, the veterans of past years tell her. *Just wait until we clean out the bottoms of the incubators. Then you'll see some freaks. Fish with two heads!*

Pam snaps on her light and pushes up her sleeves. She scoops out one of the fry and holds it gently under the magnifying lens. Then, slipping the points of the circumcision scissors between the opaque pair of fins on its belly, she snips away the right one. The fry twitches between her fingers as she makes the cut, and then lies still. She drops it into the recovery bucket and picks up the next fish.

Fin-marking seems to Pam to be, at once, primitively barbaric and modernly scientific. Such maiming, she's been told, is the only tested method biologists know to permanently identify populations of salmon fry. Once they know what portion of a population is marked, they can use the number of marked fish recovered as adults to determine ocean survival rates. Different combinations of fin clips—right ventral alone, or adipose and left ventral, or both ventrals together—can be used to identify separate stocks or the same stock released at different times or in different places.

Pam eases back into the repetitive motion. She's skillful, with so much practice, at quickly separating the tissuey ventral fins and cleanly amputating the right one. With each good clip, she feels the slight resistance of the cartilage at the fin's base. If the cut isn't close enough, the fin will rejuvenate; too close and the fish will die.

Staring through the magnifying glass at her enlarged fingers curled lightly around the slack bit of fish, Pam fills her head with pictures of parading salmon heading to the freedom of the sea, flagging their fins as they push themselves along. Dorsal, adipose, pectoral, ventral, anal, and caudal—she names the fins. Anything to clutter her head, to keep her from thinking of the shovels digging into sand, turning up bones.

She didn't know Roni all that well back in Oregon, not until near the end of their senior year. Each had her own way of dealing with the constraints of small-town life. Roni threw herself into jazz dancing and the school's drama productions. Pam bided her time more quietly, reading nineteenth-century novels and taking walks in the rain. Neither made any secret of her intention to leave town for distant and more adventurous parts as soon as school was over. While the others talked about heading to the state university or looking for local jobs, Pam and Roni separately settled on Alaska. Once that was decided, it made sense for them to team up for the trip. Each of their families reluctantly agreed to their going, as long as they were to be together.

In Anchorage, they looked for work. Roni dragged Pam along to her first interview, urging her to apply as well. "A dancer?" Pam said. "You've got to be kidding. What kind of dancing?" She pictured some sort of chorus line act, costumes decorated with spangles and plumes.

"The easy kind. Just moving to the music."

Pam wasn't impressed when she saw the place. On the outside it looked like a tacky bar making just half an effort, with a bunch of neon tubing, to look like a nightclub. *Girls Girls Girls*, it said, with a picture of a martini glass. Inside, Pam read *Topless–Bottomless* in the entryway while Roni announced her appointment with the manager. They were asked to sit at a table to wait.

The room was dark and smelled of stale smoke and disinfectant. Chairs were overturned on the tables. All the furniture and paneling were wood or a wood-grained plastic, and western paintings and manufactured oxen yokes decorated the walls. There was a stage set up for a band and several platforms for the dancers.

"Cowboy," Roni said, looking around.

"Are you sure you want to do this?" Pam asked. "I mean, won't you feel self-conscious, without any clothes on?"

"No." Roni smiled, her face set in innocence. "What are you gonna do—tell my parents?" She flipped her long hair back behind one ear. "It's not like I know anyone. Geez, the only person I know in the whole state is you. C'mon, why don't you try out too? It would be a kick. We could just do it for a while, until we saved up some money, and then we could go gold mining or something."

The manager came out and talked to Roni for a few minutes. He led her away to change, and then he dropped a quarter into the jukebox and sat with Pam while Roni danced through his selection of songs. The outfit he'd given her was pretty skimpy—just some fringe strung together. Pam watched him as he watched Roni; his dark eyes stayed on her steadily and his mouth kept its small, rather feminine pucker of concentration. When the music stopped, he got up and walked over to her. Pam couldn't hear what they said, but she saw Roni flash a smile.

Pam had to admit eventually that it didn't seem to be such a bad job for Roni. She just danced, without paying any attention to the men who looked up at her between swigs of their beer. She didn't have to mingle with them or get within their reach. And besides, Roni kept reminding her, it was different in Alaska. You could do anything. Attitudes were a lot freer and standards looser. *This is Alaska!* she and Roni told each other, back and forth.

Pam took a job waitressing, but she still had a vague notion of wanting to do something outdoors—planting trees or cooking at a wilderness lodge, anything to get out beyond the mountains that circled the city. After a couple of weeks she packed her things and headed down the coast. When she resumed waitressing, it was in a fishing town where everyone wore rubber boots and the cafe was filled every morning with the same group of men who helped themselves to the coffee. Moving back and forth with their orders, Pam listened to the snippets of talk about fish prices and rogue waves, newly hung gear and long-ago record catches. They spoke of an Alaska where spawning salmon jammed the creeks so tightly a person could walk across their backs, where dozens of bears lined up along the falls to fish. Pam felt herself drawn to the wildness that supported, like the framework of boasts, the table talk.

It was hard to keep in touch with Roni when neither of them had phones. Still, Pam felt a strong tie between them. Their shared escape to Alaska and their time together in Anchorage had cemented what might not have existed otherwise as an actual friendship into something even more solid. As different as they might be in some ways, there was something—Pam thought of it as some basic sharing of *soul*—that held them to one another. They phoned each other at work, grabbing a few minutes before one or the other was called away. There was never enough time to get caught up the way Pam felt they needed to. Roni said she still enjoyed dancing. "A while longer," she said. "Then I'll be ready for another kind of adventure. Get me a job on one of those fishing boats."

In August, Pam was hired at the hatchery as part of a crew to do "egg takes." It was temporary, for just a few weeks, but it was a chance at last to leave the town behind and see the country beyond. Flying out, she marveled at the stretches of forest and muskeg and the sandy braids of long river valleys. Wrapped in rain gear, the crew netted salmon into pens, clubbed them, and stripped them of their eggs and milt. The eggs, spilling into buckets, shone like pink pearls.

When she got back to town, Pam called Roni.

"She doesn't work here anymore," whoever answered said.

Pam insisted on speaking to the manager.

"She didn't show up one night," he said, "and we haven't heard from her since. We got her stuff here. One of the girls brought it from her place. Let her know we got her stuff if you see her."

Pam talked to the police after that. Yes, she'd been reported missing. No, they had no leads. No, they hadn't tried to find her. They weren't staffed to chase down every missing person. No, they didn't think they'd talked to her family.

Pam called her own parents and they called Roni's. Then Pam found herself on the phone with Roni's father.

"What kind of establishment was this that she was working at?" he asked.

"A bar," Pam said.

"A bar." Pam heard him draw a breath. "She told me she was waitressing. Don't they have laws up there against eighteen-year-olds serving liquor?"

Pam was silent, remembering Roni's taunt. *What are you gonna do—tell my parents?* The best she could do was try to put it in a good light. "Her job was as a dancer."

"A dancer?" His voice rose in pitch, and Pam could hear another voice in the background, a woman's, but she couldn't hear the words or tell the tone.

"A dancer," Pam said. She pictured Roni in one of the school productions, tap dancing her way across the stage, dressed in a tuxedo-like costume. She willed the wholesome pictures to the minds of her parents. "On a stage," she said. "She was above—everyone."

The next day Pam met Roni's father at the Anchorage airport. "You didn't tell me what kind of place it was," he said as they drove to the police station.

"I told you it was a bar," Pam said.

"The police told me it was a lot more than that."

Pam was silent.

"It's a strip joint. You knew that, didn't you?"

Pam looked at his hard, worn face. She could tell he was envisioning the worst—some horrid place where drunken perverts fondled themselves and yelled obscenities at the women. "It's not like that," she said. "It's different. This is Alaska." She could see that he didn't understand. "It's not like anywhere else. She liked to dance, and it was okay."

Roni's father looked at her sharply. "They're prostitutes. They take drugs."

At the police station they went through the box of Roni's things. Nothing seemed to be missing. They both answered more questions for a young cop. "She talked about going gold mining or fishing," Pam said. "No, she wouldn't have gone without telling me. No, she never mentioned a boyfriend."

Pam looks up as Doug lifts the plastic flap and enters with his sample cups.

"How're you gals doing?" he yells above all the noise.

They nod and smile as they continue fin-marking. Doug dips into each of their buckets for his samples and takes them off to the lab. Partly, Pam knows, the checks under the microscope are to make sure the clippers are doing a good job. But beyond that, the checks help them figure the percentages that can be expected to either grow back their fins or die, so that can be plugged into the statistics.

One at a time, the women are called to the lab to get their reports. Pam is glad for the break.

Doug has three of her fish separated in a small bowl. "They're pretty good," he says. "Your speed's good too, so I don't think you're compromising either way. I want you to take a look at a couple of them, though." He scoops one onto a slide and adjusts the microscope. "Here," he says, moving away so that Pam can look. "Use this tweezer to pull back the fin."

Under magnification the texture of the fish skin reminds Pam of the webs of tiny lines on the back of her hands. With the point of tweezer, she lifts the left ventral fin clear. Opposing it, a thin remnant of the right fin lies against the body. The scissor cut looks like an angled slice through a slab of meat.

"See it?" Doug asks. "There's a couple like that. It looks like you came in at an off angle and so missed getting it clean. Watch that you keep the scissor angle close to the body. Let's get this baby back into some water." He dumps the fry back and fishes out another. He pushes it around on the slide and refocuses. "That's the other one. Look at that."

Pam can see right away where the body is cut—a spooned-out hollow behind the fin.

"That one won't live," Doug says. "It's only one out of twenty—five percent—but try to be a little more careful. And don't be squeamish. If you know you got one too close . . ." He picks up the fish and cuts neatly through it with a pair of scissors, dropping the two halves to the table. "Keep it out of the statistics. You're doing good, though. Keep it up."

Pam clips for another half hour, and then they're all called to lunch. Because it's warm and sunny, Jake has decided they'll have a cookout, and he's grilling hamburgers over a charcoal fire. "In honor of the ladies," he says. "The pale, pale ladies with the cold hands."

The crew stands around the fire, watching the meat sizzle and dodging the smoke. "Smoke follows beauty," someone says as Jake, coughing, twists away from where he squats to turn the burgers.

Pam digs in the cooler for a soft drink. Burgers and chips—that's what they get when the men cook. But they're all good people, and they all get along in the way people do who live and work so closely together.

A helicopter flies low down the river valley. Whup-whup-whup. As it passes almost over the hatchery, the spinning blades are deafening, and the crew looks up, squinting into the sun. Then it's behind the hill, the clatter muted as it heads toward Anchorage.

Someone says it. "Going back in the middle of the day—they must have found something."

No one says anything after that. Pam, staring into the fire, can feel them watching her. She pictures it again, a shovel turning up bones, a long leg bone slender and white. Bones being shoveled into a bag. Sand being sifted for bits of cloth, bullets, an earring.

Pam lifts her face to the sun as she tips her soft drink back. When she closes her eyes to the glare, she sees only the deep red of the inside of her eyelids.

Last summer, when she was first hired for the egg-take, Pam had reveled in the country and its remoteness. Splashing around with the fish, watching the morning fogs burn off into sun-drenched days, hiking to an unnamed lake that hung in an alpine valley like a turquoise stone, waiting out the storms that threatened to flood the hatchery or leave them short of supplies–they were all parts of the wildness that she'd craved. *This is Alaska!*

The bear had been part of that, too. One evening at the edge of dusk, when the sky had faded to a soft blue over the treetops, she was walking along the creek when a black bear pushed from the woods into her path. It stopped and rose to its hind legs, its nose in the air as though it were looking out over the top of bifocals. Its paws hung on limp wrists against its chest, and Pam could see–she was that close– the long claws that curved to points. She remembered the magazine picture that someone, as an amusement, had tacked to the hatchery bulletin board. It was of a man who had recovered from being mauled by a bear; his head was misshapen and raised with scars, and one eye was permanently sealed.

The bear shook its head back and forth a few times, clicked its teeth, and coughed into a growl. Then it dropped to the ground and sauntered off in the direction it had been headed when it emerged from the trees. Its smell, like sweaty socks, hung in the air behind it; Pam sucked at it with heart-pounding breaths, thrilled with the narrowness of the margin between them there on the trail, between the wild and the tamed, between life and death.

She thought of Roni, then, wanting to share it with her. Roni would appreciate it as she appreciated the brutishness of Anchorage. Roni laughed at the city's stylish pretensions–the tall glass buildings, the restaurants with their velveteen chairs and bow-tied waiters, the theater company that ordered its costumes from Europe. It was the Natives drinking from paper-sacked bottles in the alleys that interested her, and the bearded men who laid their easy money on a game of pool and bought drinks for the house. If there was a risk there, living on that edge, that only enhanced her interest in it. Anyone could live comfortably in a settled place—but what kind of life was that for the two of them? Neither of them had fled the safe, well-traveled streets of their hometown just to shy away from what they found in this new and boundless land.

No one mentions the air traffic or the search effort again during the lunch break. The women file back to their seats in the hatchery and, as Doug weighs their marked fish from the morning for a count, they resume clipping.

Linda Ronstadt is singing again, on the tape deck. In her head, Pam sings along with "Tracks of My Tears." Her motions, one fish to the next, are as fluid as the music, or as the water spilling through the raceways.

Pam sees the river in sunlight, rolling over rapids and swirling through eddies, and then a plane parked on a sandbar. Roni, admiring the view from beside the plane, listens to the rush of water. She holds her arms wide, twirling in a circle; perhaps she says something to the man who has flown her there. *All this! To think I might have stayed in Oregon and not known.* Then, the grip of his hand on her arm. The look in his eye. The gun, as he slowly, systematically, loads it.

Pam feels the crunch of cartilage and the tremble of the fish body as she cuts too closely. She tilts the bit of silver back and forth beneath the magnifying glass to view the impression she left.

Roni, running across the sand, runs for her life.

The bear—when it stood before Pam, sniffing the air—she was able to imagine the rip of its claws. For seconds, she felt the possibility. Then, as she watched it amble off, she breathed its musk and was still alive; she'd never really thought it could be otherwise. Roni, meanwhile, witnessed the beer brawls, the drunken cowboys as they were helped to the door; perhaps, with time, she learned to recognize the regulars, to identify types and individuals. In their turn, the drunks, the brawlers, and the quiet, inoffensive drinkers watched her. Eagerly she would accept a plane ride, intent on the country, the height, the wind, the closeness of valley walls and spiring spruce as she flew over them.

Pam sees Roni falling, crumpling into an awkward, artless heap.

The limp fish body rests on her forefinger, the tiny gills pumping air with a barely perceptible movement. It won't live, and yet, perhaps . . . She draws her scissors away and, slowly, lowers the marked fish to the bucket.

The Lady with the Sled Dog

They were saying she was here, waiting. The secretaries were calling her the lady with the sled dog, although *lady* was not a word in their vocabularies. Grove, who was assigned the interview, thought they only said it for his benefit, to tease him. He was so old-fashioned, he sometimes forgot and used *lady* as a term of respect.

The secretaries were looking smug. They all knew that the lady with the sled dog had mushed her team over a thousand miles of frozen mountains, through blizzards and darkness. She'd outdistanced all the men in the Alaskan race and set a new record to boot. Now she was touring the country, giving interviews.

Grove didn't like dogs. He didn't like snow, cold, or sleeplessness, and he wasn't sure he liked women. He was curious about what sort of woman lived in Alaska with a pack of dogs. She would not be the same kind who lived in Baltimore, he felt sure.

She was waiting for him in the interview room, with her dog. The dog stood up when he opened the door. He hesitated. Dogs didn't like him any more than he liked *them*. The dustmop variety was always dashing out from under furniture and biting his ankles; big dogs, at least, were less surreptitious. This one stretched itself like a wolf. It was dark gray except for cream-colored markings on its face and chest, markings that highlighted its eyebrows and made it look like it was wearing a V-neck sweater.

He apologized for being late.

"You're right on time," she said, and laughed. "We walked around the block twice, but we were still early."

Grove looked at his watch to avoid staring at her. She wasn't what he had expected. Her sun-streaked hair fell in a thick braid across one shoulder, and her face was clear, with fine, china-doll features and blue eyes. She was wearing a long, crimson dress belted at an impossibly thin waist. She couldn't have weighed much more than a hundred pounds.

"Let's get started," he said. He moved away from the dog, toward the opposite chair. The dog watched him. Its eyes were even lighter than its mistress's, silver, like metal washers. Grove flipped his notebook open. He had no idea what to ask, so he asked her how many dogs she had.

"A hundred and forty."

He looked up at her, unsure if he'd heard right. *A hundred* and forty?

"Some are puppies, of course," she said. "You have to raise and train a lot of dogs in order to have enough to put together a top team. Melon here's one of my oldest dogs. She ran the Iditarod five times, but she's retired now. Aren't you, girl?" she said, hugging the dog to her side. "A well-earned retirement."

The dog stretched its neck, closed its eyes to slits, and smiled. Grove had never seen a dog smile before, had not known it was possible. The corners of the dog's grizzled mouth actually curled up.

"Yes," Grove said, writing *140 . . . Melon . . . retired . . . smile.*

She went on, telling him how she trained her dogs, worked with each puppy, ran teams all summer over the bare ground with a wheeled chassis instead of a sled. She told him how she culled out the ones that slacked off, kept the ones that took the weight. She reached into a crocheted bag and pulled out a bright purple bundle of nylon straps and began to fit it over the dog. It was Melon's harness, she explained. Her long, bare hands were practiced and sure, loving as they tugged and stroked. The dog shivered with pure joy.

Grove was making notes, but he was thinking about his wife. Her hands were liver-spotted and rough, sharp-boned, like the feet of a hawk. He pictured them gripping the potato masher, the knuckles white and angry, or steering the vacuum cleaner, molded to it like more cold plastic. Her hands grabbed and clutched, did chores to get them done. He supposed they were practiced in their own way, just not at eliciting that sort of response. She didn't touch him. No, of course she did; sometimes in bed they clung like orphans to each other. She squeezed his backside in her fists. But that was not the same.

"Melon," he said. The dog snapped its head toward him as though it thought it was being called. Grove looked away. "Is that one L or two?"

"Like the fruit," she said.

"Isn't that an odd name?" He was careful not to repeat it, not to attract any more of the dog's attention.

She bobbed her head and explained that she'd gotten the dog from a man who named his litters by categories. Melon came from a litter of fruit—Apple, Berry, Guava, Peaches. She said she did the same thing with her pups. Her last three litters were storms, trees, and junk foods. She rattled off names.

The dog was wagging its tail. Grove envied its enthusiasm. Pat it, say its name, put some straps around its chest and over its back, and it was in dog heaven. The dog loved her, and it loved to run for her. He was sure of it. The dog ran for love. And no wonder.

She was going on and on, telling him about how carefully she managed the dogs' diets.

He interrupted. "Are you happy?"

Her eyes opened wider and their blue seemed to reach back into her head. He felt as though he were standing at the bottom of a pool and looking up toward light.

"Of course," she said. "Aren't you?"

He hadn't known he wasn't, not for sure, until that moment. He had nothing to complain about. Job, family, friends, a good meal, the sound of an oboe well played—these were ordinary satisfactions, perhaps even moments of happiness. But they didn't add up.

He asked her to tell him more about racing—about the big race, the Iditarod, a thousand miles of trail.

She told him about winning, about strategy, about sleeplessness, and about knowing the dogs so well you know exactly what to expect from them and how much to ask them for. She talked about the days of pushing the sled over hummocks and through heavy snow, the nights of running under starlight.

"You have your team," she said, "and you're all together like parts of the same organism. And then you've got the country, as big and empty as anywhere in the world. At night, when the mountains are lit by the moon and stars, and it's about thirty degrees below zero, and maybe a few northern lights are twisting away in the sky"—she drew a breath—"it gets you right here." She bounced her fingers against her chest. "I feel funny talking about it, but it's religious, that's all I can say."

Grove shut his eyes. He could see a pale world, luminous mountains backing away from each other, starlight catching on the brittle grains of snow. He thought he understood. It's what he wanted, too—a world so clean and quiet and beautiful, it would make you want to cry.

He opened his eyes. The dog was watching him, its ghostly silver eyes staring as though waiting for him to give a command. Grove held out his hand. The dog nuzzled it and crept closer. He placed his hand on the dog's neck. The fur was soft, soft and warm. The dog turned its head and licked the back of his hand.

Grove thought his heart would break.

Grove wrote the story about the lady with the sled dog. He mentioned the training and the diets and the Iditarod race. He described the country as empty and cold, the nights lit by stars. He didn't say anything about religion.

The article came out with a couple of pictures from the press packet, showing the sled, showing her cutting frozen meat with an axe.

Grove lived his life as before. He stopped at the market to buy milk, played some tennis, took his car to the garage to have it inspected, did his work, offered to help his wife with the vacuuming. She cooked chicken with an orange sauce, his favorite, and wore a new nightgown. The streets were dusty; it rained or it didn't rain. Winter came, and it was cold, for Baltimore.

Sometimes, late at night, he sat in his chair in the living room and thought about the lady with the sled dog. He remembered her hands and the way she slipped the harness over the dog, her eyes and how they'd widened with surprise. When he woke up at night, he stared at the dark ceiling and thought he saw stars, thought he heard the glide of sled runners over snow.

He rearranged his chair to face north.

He made his plans at the last minute, and so, when he got off the plane in Anchorage, the race was already beginning downtown. Grove—outfitted in a goose-down parka, the copy editor's après-ski boots, and a fur hat he'd found at the Army-Navy, a tall hat he thought looked Russian—caught a taxi.

Snow had been trucked in for the race, laid on the streets to make a track. They were starting the teams at two-minute intervals, amid a terrific din of cheering and barking. Grove hadn't known there were so many people in Alaska or that they took dogsled racing so seriously. He started at the front and worked his way through the crowd, elbowing aside photographers, craning past small children who sat on their fathers' shoulders. He was running out of time.

He found her, not far from the starting gate. She looked different; she was wearing a fat yellow snowsuit and a wool hat, with goggles resting on her forehead. Her dogs—a long string of them—were paired two and two and two out in front of the sled. Some swung their tails about and bit at the air, while others simply sat and waited. One opened its mouth wide, showing all its teeth, and yawned a cloud of frosted breath. She was moving up the line, checking their harnesses, saying something to one, leaning down to rub another on the head. He could tell: she loved every dog, every dog loved her.

And then it was her turn to move into position. She ran back and stood on the sled runners. Handlers led the team to the gate.

Grove followed along, forcing his way through the crowd, trying to keep her in sight. The shouting and whistling swelled to a roar; children clapped their thick, muffled mitten-hands. He pushed a-head, came even with some of her dogs. He stretched his neck to see past a fur-trimmed hood, between a video camera and a raised fist. For a second her face filled the space, aglow with purpose and, yes, happiness. And then she was off, the dogs leaping forward, a pack of raw energy.

Grove yelled with the rest. "Melon!" is what he shouted. "Go, Melon, go!" And then he remembered that Melon was retired. Melon wasn't on the team.

The lady with the sled dog, with all the sled dogs, was off on a thousand-mile journey. In a short time, all the noise would be behind them, and they would enter that perfect white world. And it seemed to him, as he stood there and could no longer see them, that his whole long trail was barely beginning.

A Guy Like Me

The first thing Althea wants, after we're walking back in the main part of town, just walking like a couple of people – the tall skinny dude that's me, and her, that looks like she might be my little sister but not my girlfriend which I guess is what she is, my girlfriend – is to eat. "We'll go to Dino's," she says, like it's already decided, and she skips over the sidewalk.

Dino's has steaks and a salad bar. It's the nicest place we ever ate. But I don't feel like eating, not now. It surprises me that she does, but then people react different and I don't know her that well yet. It's five weeks since we started hanging around together. I'm starting to see that she's hard, like she could be made from concrete.

Me, I don't even want to *think* about eating. I'm not feeling so good overall. Maybe I want to have a couple beers, some cigarettes. Unwind, like they say, after a hard day. If I go in a restaurant, it would just be to wash my hands.

"C'mon, Willy," she says, pulling on my arm to make me walk faster. "I ain't had but that old cereal this morning, and potato chips." When she lets go of me, she pats the upper pocket of her jean jacket, proud. It bulges, almost like she's got a breast under there instead of being flat-chested. I think she wouldn't look bad if she did have breasts and got that hair off her face where it slicks down to the top of her eyes. I tell her it makes her look like she's trying to hide under it, like it was a hat she could pull over her eyes. Aside from that, I tell her, it'll give you pimples, greasy hair on your face like that. I'm sensitive about pimples, cause I used to have wicked ones that left these scars all over my face. Right now she's got smooth skin like a little kid, but it could be she could still get pimples. That's what I like about her is that skin. All smooth and soft on the outside, covering that concrete. That, and she doesn't care if I did have pimples.

"You had a Pepsi too," I remind her.

"You don't *eat* Pepsis," she says.

They say when you start screwing, that's when you get rid of pimples. That just shows you how unfair life is. No one wants to screw you when you've got pimples, so how are you supposed to get rid of them? If it's true, though, maybe I'm doing her a favor and she'll never have the problem. Although I don't think she needed me for that.

I stop to light cigarettes, one for each of us, turning toward a tree and cupping the match out of the wind. While I'm doing that, I see her unbutton her pocket and pull a bill off the roll. She stuffs it in another pocket and rebuttons the one over the roll. Dinner money, so she doesn't have to do it later when there's people watching. She's smart, sometimes, like that.

Other times, she's not so smart. She does what she wants, without thinking about it. Then, later, it's too late. I don't know—when I was fourteen I wasn't so smart either. Lucky is what I was. There's something about when you're so little, no one can believe you can be so bad. That's what that man thought, seeing that angelface in his door.

Standing behind, off to the side, I couldn't see what Althea looked like but I could imagine. I could see the old guy, every expression his face went through, all in a few seconds. She talked soft, and he leaned over, like to hear what kind of cookies she was selling. Old guy like that, he was probably deaf anyway.

Then I saw his face, when she pointed the gun at him, go sort of surprised, then almost smiling, like he thought it was funny, then kind of strict like he was going to say, "Don't ever point a gun, not even a toy one." I saw his hand come up and push the barrel aside. She fired, right into the floor. There wasn't anything for me to do then but push in behind for backup.

So we go to Dino's, just the way she wants. We order steaks and baked potatoes and then go through the salad bar. None of it looks good to me. I make myself take some lettuce, some of those brown nutlike things, seeds, shredded carrot. There's beets, cut with frills like potato chips, but I skip over them and the rest. Althea's on the other side, taking some of everything, heaping her plate until it looks like some of it might start rolling off. She ladles on a bunch of green dressing. Her hair's falling in her eyes, so she keeps tossing her head. I'm embarrassed it's so dirty, it sticks together like it's one piece.

We sit down at a booth in the corner. I look at that salad in front of me and my stomach draws up tight, like if it had hands it would jerk them out and push the plate away. I smoke a cigarette.

Althea eats, though, leaning over her plate, with that green dressing all over the corners of her mouth. "Jesus," I say. "You look like a orphan that's been starved. Why don't you sit back? And wipe your mouth." It's the first thing I've said to her since we got in the restaurant. She picks up her napkin from under her other fork and dabs at her mouth with a show like she's a lady.

I don't know what she's thinking about, if she's just doing it to be cute, but I can see that other napkin, back at the house, as she went through the lady's purse. Just like a pro, she took a cloth napkin from the dinner table and held it in her hand while she unsnapped the lady's pocketbook, picked out the wallet, opened it, pulled out all the bills. That's another way she's smart—knowing not to leave fingerprints. I think she learned that from the TV.

"Ain't you gonna eat?" she says.

I put my cigarette out and pick up my fork. I eat some of the lettuce and chew on one of those little squares of toast. I know I'm hungry. At least I should be. The last thing I had was potato chips in the afternoon, the same as her. Still, it's hard to swallow. I can chew all right, but it's like my stomach's saying, "You stay up there in the mouth. I don't want food down here right now."

So I chew a whole bunch more and look off around the room, trying to take my mind off everything. There are all kinds of people in here, eating and drinking and being happy with their lives. Right next to us is this big guy, looks like he could be a football player, with a blond girl. They're so nice looking, they could be in a commercial for anything you wanted. The guy has on a dark green sweater, the color of a forest. The girl's real slim, but with a nice figure, not straight like Althea. She's wearing a sweater too, with reindeer on it. Those are nice tits pushing out the front of it and nice legs crossed under the table. I think about how she goes together with that big guy. She'd want to be on top. With a guy like me, she wouldn't get squished anyway.

I'm listening hard to what they say, so that I can try to swallow. They're talking about other people and what they'll buy someone for a present. They sound like that's the biggest worry they ever had —what to get someone for a present—and I start to get mad. How come they can be beautiful and rich and have friends to give presents to? They look like they always have anything they ever want. How come? I'd like to be able to walk up to a girl like that and tell her to come live with me. Aren't I just as good as that guy? Couldn't I do the same job he does, if someone would just show me how, say "Yes, sir" to me once in my life?

I don't even hear when they call our number. "That's us, dummy," Althea says, kicking me under the table. She thinks that's something I should do, go up to the counter and get the plates, like it's man's work. Like we're on a date, maybe. I slide out of the booth and go up. I never know for sure when she wants me to do something that seems like the man's job, and when she wants to do it herself. It seems like, if it's pretty boring, like going to the counter for food or popping a lock, she wants me to do it. If there's more excitement to it, like rolling one of the downtown drunks or carrying a gun, that's what she likes to do herself.

I'm still thinking this when I bring the plates to the table. She laughs. "What's the matter with you?" she says. "Here I am takin' you out to eat and you don't even appreciate it."

I could get mad, with that kind of attitude, but those other people are still sitting next to us. Even, I notice, their legs are touching under the table, rubbing together. Althea thinks she's taking me to dinner, thinks the money's hers. If she wasn't so dumb, we could have had a lot more than that. That house was full of it. Even the ring on that lady's finger, that was a diamond as big as they come. I sit down hard. "Later," I say.

Althea's already sawing away on her steak and doesn't see the look I give her. The blood gushes out of her steak, pooling up under her potato, and I have to look away. My own is much better done. I trim off the fat and cut a couple pieces. I chew but my stomach still doesn't want to swallow. Althea slugs at her Pepsi to wash a mouthful down. In a way I envy her, but it doesn't seem right that she should be able to enjoy it so much when I'm just as hungry and want it the same. She messed up, and I'm the one that can't eat.

The people next to us finally leave. I just know they'll be screwing within ten minutes. She has a real nice ass, I see when she gets up.

Althea wipes up the last of the steak blood on her plate.

"You can have some of mine," I say.

She belches, without even turning her head. "I'm full," she says.

"I'll get a doggy bag to take it," I say.

"Hell, no," she says, reaching across and stabbing one of the pieces I'd cut. "When you're hungry we'll just buy some more. I'm not gonna go walkin' down the street with you carryin' one of them little white bags. They got a picture of a poodle dog on the outside."

"So what," I say. I'm not leaving it, not after we paid for it. Not after the money came that way.

Althea places her hand over her pocket. It's hot in the restaurant, but she's never taken off that jacket. Even if she didn't have the money in it, that jacket is one thing she always wears. It's too big for her, more like a man's size—my size, maybe, although I never tried it on. I think she feels like she can hide in it, like it's some kind of armor to protect her, or maybe it just makes her feel bigger.

Anyway, she puts her hand over the pocket. It looks funny, like if it was a boob there she'd be feeling herself up. It makes me think of that girl again. Her hair was so clean it swung over her shoulders, when she got up, like some kind of shiny, silky material that could be on the bottom of a curtain. So why can't I have a girl like that, instead of this titless one that can't even keep herself clean and has bones sticking out where there's supposed to be curves?

"Don't you want to know how much?" Althea asks. She's rubbing her hand around over her pocket.

"No," I say, feeling real nervous about what other people might see. I lean across the table. "If you take that out . . ." but I don't know how to finish. It's like I'm with my little brothers again, threatening

them with broken bones and wrung necks—things I'd never even do
to a bird. "You wait," I say. "That would be real dumb."

"I wasn't gonna do anything, you idiot," she spits back at me. "It
happens I already know. You probably didn't think of that—that I'd
be smart enough to count it when I took it."

I didn't figure on that. I knew I was always too nervous and in too
much hurry to bother counting. "How much?" I ask.

"I'm not gonna tell you," she says, dropping her hand and turning
sideways in the booth with a snooty face, her pointed chin tipped up
in the air.

I lean back against the fake leather. "So what do you want to do
now?"

"Can't you let me digest?" she says. She waits a minute, then she
says, "I'm thinkin' about what I'll buy."

I know she's just saying that to give me a hard time, to make me
want to ask her again about the money, how much there is. She
doesn't think about how she'll spend money. She just spends it when
she has it. She'll walk in some store and buy something she thinks is
cute. There was this giraffe she liked last week—a stuffed thing with a
long neck. She bought it, then she left it somewhere a couple days
later and never went back for it. It's like she just wanted it right then.
She would never buy something useful, like underwear.

I scratch the side of my face. "What are you gonna buy?"

She looks around the emptying room, sailing her eyes across the
colored glass lights and the hanging plants. She settles on a group of
people seated at a table in the center. "I want some boots like that."
She points. One of the ladies is wearing shiny gray boots with tall,
spiked heels.

I can't hardly picture her in those, or in anything except the blue
and white running shoes she always wears. "You'd fall on your face,"
I say.

"I wouldn't," she says.

"How're you gonna run, then?"

"I'll get someone to drive me," she says. "I'll take a cab."

"Yeah, like tonight," I say. "I s'pose you'd call a cab from that
house."

I'm sorry right away I said it. It's just, I know she doesn't care
about boots with high heels, it's just what she saw when she looked

around. I don't want the money to go like that, for nothing. It seems like, this time, no matter how much it is, it's worth more. I'd rather stretch it out, buying food and stuff, so we don't have to do it like that again.

I rub my hands over my eyes. When I look through my fingers I see she's just sitting there, laying back in the booth like she's trying to take pressure off her stomach. She's not looking at me or anything but she doesn't look sad either.

"Gimme a cigarette," she says, when she sees I'm watching her.

I toss the whole pack over to her. I know before she even lights up that she'll blow smoke in my face. It must mean I'm starting to understand her.

It turns out Althea has the same idea as me for once. We walk over to the Uptown Motel and get a room. It's not much of a place. The Uptown's the kind of motel that fills up when the welfare checks come out, when people can pay for a room before they go back on the street. The good thing is they don't care who you are as long as you pay in advance.

The only other thing we might have done was hang out a while and then go back to where we've been staying. It's not too great there—just an empty apartment we let ourselves into. It's real empty except for carpet, and the electric and water's turned off too, so there's nothing to do there but sleep.

Althea says she wants to go to one of the fancy hotels. I think she's half serious, maybe more. "You know, room service," she says, "where you can order up champagne and stuff in the middle of the night and you put your shoes out in the hall for them to polish."

"What's this you got about *shoes* all of a sudden?" I say, thinking again of those shiny boots that weren't the kind to be polished anyway. "How do you think that would look—you and me trying to check into a place like that?"

"We got the money," she says, sticking her little chin out like she thinks that's all there is to it.

"Yeah? Well, you got a lot to learn," I tell her. "They don't care about just *money*. You think it looks natural for a guy like me and a little girl to go walking in, say 'Give us a room with a view?' You think that wouldn't raise some eyebrows? Jail bait."

We're walking then, and we both know we're headed for the Up-town. The thing is, I really would like to stay in one of them places, just once. I could pass for the kind of dude that would. Of course I couldn't ever take Althea. She'd be a dead giveaway.

First thing I do after we get a room is take a shower. Usually, I feel that way – if I can just use enough soap I can wash away some of that feeling about having done something bad. This time I stay in a long time, and I turn the water hotter and hotter until my skin is red. I squeak my hair a hundred times, trying to feel clean.

When I'm as clean as I can get, I walk naked into the bedroom with a towel on my head. Althea's lying on the bed with both pillows behind her, watching TV. Her white socks are loose on her feet, like they're half dragged off or too big to start with – maybe mine or filched from a dryer where you take what you get. Anyway, they're pretty gray on the bottoms, like she's been wearing them a long time.

"Your turn," I say. I start drying my hair with the towel, standing there in the middle of the room.

"It's *Beverly Hills Cop*," she says. She doesn't take her eyes off the TV. "Someone's gotta go down and get more quarters. I only got two more."

I sit next to her, on the edge of the bed. The mattress is so soft it makes me lean toward her, like it might fold up in the middle with us inside. Another time, I'd let myself fall into her, fooling around. Something about the way she's lying, though, with her ankles crossed and her arms folded around her, with that damn jacket still buttoned up – I can tell she just wants to watch the TV and nothing else. And I'm still not feeling so hot about the whole evening. So I hold myself on the edge and look at the TV too, how it's all bolted together up near the ceiling so you can't steal it. Up in the air like that is how they are in detention centers, prisons, places like that, only that's so people won't kick them or fight about the channels.

It must be a movie channel, cable, she's watching, to have a movie that good. It's near the end, when the kid cop stands up and waves his badge around, telling everyone they're under arrest. I remember, at the movies, everyone laughed then. It was a big joke, that the dumb

young cop would think that everyone played by the rules, that all
you had to do was tell them what the law was and they'd do it.

Everyone's shooting and getting shot. It's all the way it is in movies and on TV. The guy who's shot flops down, maybe with some red
dye on his shirt. I remember what's coming—Eddie Murphy and the
bad guy in the house, trying to kill each other. When Eddie Murphy
gets him cornered, he shoots him about a million times.

I look at Althea. She's just sitting there like it's a cartoon, fake
animals jumping off cliffs or blowing each other up. "You ever seen
this before?" I ask.

"Of course," she says.

Of course, like I'm a dummy not to know. I'm supposed to know
everything, I guess. It just seems weird to me, that she wants to sit
there and watch all that killing right now. I go in the bathroom and
put some of my clothes on, then I sit on the closed toilet lid and
smoke cigarettes until it's over.

Later I go out and bring back a case of beer and more cigarettes. I
figure the only thing is to get real drunk. I won't sleep unless I pass
out.

Althea keeps pumping quarters into the TV, even after she stops
watching it and sits against the wall, drinking with me. She says she
likes to have the sound of it. It's like company, she tells me, so you
don't feel alone, but you also don't have to hear anything else like
people screwing next door or fighting in the hall. "I get that from my
mom," she says. "She always had the TV on. All them faces was like
my family to me. I used to think those women winning all the prizes,
that they would adopt me, take me home with their new cars and
furniture."

Althea never talks about her mother, so I'm surprised when she
does. I don't even know who Althea is or where she comes from,
except for she started showing up a few months back, and when I
asked her she said she was on her own since her mother got a new
boyfriend and baby. She told me, the first time, she was sixteen. I
knew it was a lie. Later she said she's fourteen but she feels like sixteen, like she'll be getting gray hair any day.

"So how come you left your mother?" I say.

She shrugs, takes another swallow of beer. "Wasn't like I had a choice," she says.

"How come there wasn't a choice?" I'm feeling sort of sweet toward her, like I might reach over and tuck some of her hair behind her ear so I can see more of her face.

"How come you're not with *your* mother?" she says. She's like a cat again, getting her back up, looking like she could spit at me.

"I'm a grown man," I say, "for one thing. There's a lot of difference between you and a guy like me. Besides, I go see them when I'm in the neighborhood. I lean on my brothers to keep them in line."

Mostly, what I don't tell her, the hard part was having my ma all the time fretting. I can see her face like she was here, long and sad with tired eyes, and words coming out of her mouth—"What am I gonna do with you, Willy?"

We drink and listen to the TV. It's another movie, with a lot of sirens in it.

"You got brothers and sisters?" I ask.

"Just that baby. Something's wrong with him."

"What's wrong with him?"

"Something, he was born that way. So why don't you shut up about it?"

So I shut up about it. I want to drink and talk and not listen to the TV or my own head that's thundering the words in my ears, now that I started it— *What am I gonna do with you, Willy?*

The thing my mother never understood about me was I never meant to be bad or get in that kind of trouble. It was like, the other guys were going somewhere so I went too. Then, there I was, in a car that was hot. Or I saw something I wanted more than the person that had it, so I took it. I sure never meant to hurt anyone.

Althea gets up and goes in the bathroom. I hear water running and figure she's taking a bath. So I get up and switch the TV to the sports channel. It's car racing. I should have been a racecar driver, I think. I should have been something. I drink more beer, watching that number seventeen, thinking maybe it could be me. I'm getting drunk and I remember I still haven't had anything to eat.

I pass out finally. At least, I don't remember anything until I wake up in a sweat. It's dark, dark as it gets in May when the curtain on the window is white and as thin as toilet paper, and everything in the room is gray without any outline. I look at myself. I'm still lying on top of the covers with my clothes on, but the TV's off and Althea's curled up under the covers on her side, with a fist next to her mouth, snoring.

I hate this kind of awake, after I've been passed out. It's not like swimming up out of a regular sleep, when it's slow and heavy and you have to push the sleep away from in front of you to get your head clear. Those are the times you don't always know where you are at first, or who you are, what it is you do. This kind of awake is so sudden and sharp. It's like snapping clear, maybe breaking out of a bubble in that sleep sea. Always I know exactly where I am and everything that's happened, same as if I never went to sleep or drank anything. I'm completely awake, like I slept off my tiredness in a hurry by being so far under.

I slip out of my jeans and get under the covers. Althea makes a noise like a sigh but she doesn't wake up. She doesn't have any clothes on, and when I hold the covers back for myself to get in, her body looks small and harmless.

So I lie there, trying to curl my own long body into the same shape as her, hoping that'll relax me. I listen to Althea's slow breathing and I push my fist against my chest to feel my own heart. It pushes back on my hand, beating hard and fast, like I'm doing speed. I don't want to think about anything else, so I just keep thinking about my heart, beating and beating. I remember from school, the pictures of the different parts of the heart, some red and some blue, the blood moving through, going to the lungs to get oxygen, going around the body. I can't help it, thinking of a hole, all the blood pumping out cause the heart still pushes even when the blood doesn't come back around. I roll over so I lie on my two fists, both of them pressing on my chest. It seems like it just makes it beat harder.

It doesn't seem right for Althea to be slow-breathing, down in a sleep like hibernation. I'd like it better if she'd jerk or whimper. It's not fair, for me to be holding onto my heart, thinking about it, while she's sleeping like an angel.

Finally I sit up and turn on the light. I light a cigarette and sit there and smoke and look at her. Her hair's still wet from her bath, and so it looks as greasy as ever. It'll dry funny too, from the way she's sleeping on it, so it'll stick up in points like punk. I look at her eyes. The lids are so thin and pale I can see tiny blue veinlines. Underneath them, her eyeballs move around, making the lids twitch as they jump back and forth. So she's dreaming after all. I want to know what.

I smoke the cigarette down first. Then I stub it out. "Althea," I say, shaking her shoulder. Her small body rocks with it. "Althea."

She snaps her eyes open, then blinks into the light. She doesn't move. "What?"

"What were you dreaming?"

She closes her eyes. "What you got the light on for? What're you wakin' me for?"

I say it again. "What were you dreaming?"

"Leave me alone," she says and rolls over, away from me and the light.

I shift toward her. "I thought you were having a nightmare," I say. "You were kicking and crying, making little squealing noises. You woke me up."

She doesn't say anything, and I think she's falling asleep again. Then she says, surprised, "I was?"

"Yeah. I thought you'd want me to wake you up. Don't you remember what it was?"

"Huh-uhn." She rolls onto her back, pulling the covers up tight around her neck, with little fists holding them to her. She's awake now, staring at the ceiling.

I'm thinking, the only thing I ever killed was a cat I hit when I was driving. I felt bad, so bad I stopped and drug it out of the street so it wouldn't get run over a hundred times more. It was weird seeing it, like one minute it's alive, running across the street, thinking about the kitty food waiting on the porch at home, and the next minute it's just fur with glassy eyes.

The lady, she was lying there on the floor, with her chin on a pillow I set there for her, her wrists tied behind her back and her ankles tied together too. She wasn't too happy, but it wasn't hurting her either. Althea got the money, then she walked over to where the lady was. Before I knew what she was doing, she put the gun on the back of the lady's head and fired it. Same as the cat, all of a sudden it's not there anymore, it's something dirty you don't want to touch but you feel real bad about it. I felt real bad about it. I still feel real bad about it.

"What're you thinkin' about?" Althea says.

"I'm thinking about a cat," I say.

"What cat?"

"One that was crossing the road to get its kitty food. I didn't hit it on purpose. That's the only thing I ever killed."

"You shot the old guy," she says.

It's true I shot the old guy. The way he was carrying on after the old lady, I couldn't help it. Althea didn't want to do it, like suddenly it was a man's job again.

The other truth is, the cat wasn't dead either. It was crying and digging its front claws in the cement like it would drag itself out of the road, but the back part of it was lying there not moving, flat. I ran over it again, is what I did. Put it out of its misery.

"I didn't know you would shoot the lady," I say.

"I didn't have a lot of choice," she says. "You know, I didn't have no mask. I didn't have no bandana pulled up over my nose, like you."

"You're the one said 'Look at that house hid in the trees. Let's see what's there.' When someone was home, you didn't just say 'Scuse me, I got the wrong house.' You had to pull that gun on the guy."

"They saw me up close," she says, stubborn.

"We could have changed the way you look. You know, cut your hair, dye it, put falsies on you." I think of this just as I say it, but it makes sense to me.

"They was old, anyway," she says, turning away from me, drawing herself up tighter than before. "If you're so smart . . ." she says into her pillow.

I wait for her to finish. Someone flushes a toilet somewhere and water rushes by like it's falling loose through the space behind the wall. The green bedspread, under the light, is splotchy with wear and stains, and the lines of nubbies are worn off in a lot of places. I get tired of looking at it, all the nubby lines twisting over us like a maze, and I don't think Althea's going to say any more. I never told her I was smart, anyway. When I look up, it's to see the TV looking down – the same, I think again, as how it looks down over everything in prisons.

Visqueen Winter

It was quiet again, except for the splash of Rick's shower. For about two hours every morning the trailer court was full of the sounds of cars starting up, motors racing, doors slamming, windshields being scraped, and the scrunch of ice and snow as cars backed around and lurched out onto the road. A shorter time filled with the voices of children gathering, shouting and clanking their lunch boxes as they headed to the bus. Then, as the exhaust cleared and the quiet resumed, the sky tipped toward day. Already, through the kitchen curtains, Connie could begin to make out the dull shapes of the other trailers, their blue and yellow and pink pastels as soft as clouds.

Rick scuffled into the kitchen, tying his robe around him. He sat at the table and pulled the front section of the paper toward him. Connie watched his hand come to rest beside the box with the weather summary.

"Do you want breakfast?" she asked.

Rick smoothed his wet hair back behind his ears and tugged at the ends. "I don't think so. Just juice. I need to stop and get a haircut this morning." He opened the paper and folded it back to the second page. The center of the page was filled with a blue map of Alaska. A smaller map of the rest of the country was centered below it, surrounded by a list of temperatures in all the major cities.

Connie thought it was funny—the big colored map of Alaska, the little black and white one of everywhere else. All the other maps she'd ever seen had the Lower Forty-Eight right in the middle—huge—and some miniature version of Alaska squeezed into a corner, looking like another one of the Hawaiian Islands. But there was Texas, the width of a quarter—not much bigger than that knob below Anchorage, the Kenai Peninsula.

Rick scanned the maps with a professional eye and then, with a finger following the text, read from the nation's summary. "'Windchills across New England ranged from 20 degrees below zero in southern sections to 55 below zero in northern Maine.'" He frowned. "People like to know windchills. I hate to use them 'cause they don't mean anything unless you're standing outside without any clothes on. See"—he traced his finger down the list—"the low in Boston was only seven degrees." He looked for another example. "Portland, Maine—four degrees. At least they've got weather out there."

Connie set his juice in front of him. "That's cold," she said, thinking of her great-aunt, who lived alone in an apartment in Worcester, Massachusetts. She remembered visiting there years ago, the hiss of the radiators when they went on in the morning. It was chilly even then, the heat going right through window panes that rattled in the wind. She pictured her great-aunt in one of her flowery print dresses and seamed stockings, wrapping herself in an afghan. She wasn't a woman who wore slacks. "Some people, you know, don't have all that arctic clothing. Windchill *would* make a difference."

"Yeah, well, that's what they say." Rick got up and went to get dressed. Connie leaned over the paper and looked at the temperatures for Des Moines. Fourteen to twenty-five; outlook: snow. The temperature was about the same here, but it hadn't snowed in weeks. There hadn't been any wind, either. Every day the clouds hung over Anchorage, never moving and never opening up.

Connie knew Rick would be thinking about windchill factors all day now, wondering if he used them enough. He took his job so seriously. Of course, it *was* serious—giving the weather reports on the nightly news. You wanted people to have the right information. The weather was so bad sometimes, people could die if they got lost in a storm.

Rick yelled from the bedroom, "Windchill factors are sexy."

Connie wrinkled her nose. "Where'd you get that idea?"

"You know, sexy, like people want to hear about them all the time. It's a word we use at the station. Abductions of little kids, that's sexy news. Wolf hunting, that's sexy. Working on the city's budget, that's not, that's boring."

"You guys all talk weird," Connie said.

"What do you mean?"

"Saying stuff like bad news is sexy. I think you've got one-track minds."

"I'll tell you," Rick said, coming back into the kitchen, "if we're one-track, it's on getting people to watch us. They're sitting there scarfing down dinner or with a drink in their hand, and they want the bozo on the screen to entertain them. It's not easy," he said, humping his shoulders into his coat. "Don't think it's easy getting up there night after night and trying to describe the weather so people will pay attention. Especially when the weather's not doing anything. It's not like sitting around talking to a soup can."

"Okay, okay. I'm sorry I said anything. I just meant it as a joke." Connie spun a spoon across the table. It crashed into an empty glass. "And I don't talk to soup cans."

Rick came over and bent to kiss her. "I'm sorry," he said. Connie turned her face away from him and he kissed her on the cheek. "It's just the weather. I get so much grief from everyone, as though I can do anything about it. Especially the skiers – they hate this crappy old icy stuff." He reached again to kiss Connie. "C'mon. Don't be mad."

Connie turned just enough so that their lips touched. When Rick pulled away she said, "So don't take your weather out on me. I don't much like it either."

Rick looked at his watch. "I gotta go." He pulled on his boots and made some kissing sounds from the door. "You'll do that errand for me?"

Connie nodded.

"I love you."

When he was gone Connie leaned across the table and pulled the curtain aside. Frost, wooly as bread mold, coated the metal frame along the bottom of the window, but the glass itself was clear. The light at the corner hung like a fuzzy full moon, illuminating the circle of old snow beneath it. The snow was dingy with tracked mud, sand, and ordinary city grime. Clods of filthy ice lay where they'd dropped from the bottoms of cars.

The only thing out there that was white was garbage. Connie had walked past it yesterday—the flattened styrofoam box, pale french fries trailing catsup like blood—sealed into a plate of ice by the weight and warmth of spinning tires.

It wasn't at all what she'd envisioned when Rick, triumphant, had announced his new job and asked her to go with him. From Ames, Iowa, she'd thought Alaska was exotically foreign, huge and empty except for its towering mountains and hearty Eskimos. She thought clean white snow would lie over everything, just as it buried the cornfields in winter; the difference would be its depth and the mountains sticking through.

How stupid she felt now, staring out her window at the urban dinginess. As the light grew, so too would evidence of the filth. The snow all along the road was stained yellow with dog pee; they weren't the sled dogs she had expected, but packs of dogs that ran loose, knocking over trash cans. The garbage was spread throughout the yards, pushed up against fences—newspapers, empty cans, balls of foil.

Across the way, a woman in hair curlers and a black nylon jacket bumped a cardboard box down her steps and dragged it into the shelter of the carport. The carport was wrapped around with sheets of plastic to make it into more of a garage, to give some protection to the mounds of belongings stored there. When they'd first moved to the court, Connie had been disturbed by the flap of the plastic in the wind. It was like whips lashing at her sleep, driving out the dreams.

Connie stretched out on the couch and pretended to look at the leisure section of the newspaper. She looked at the words in an article, but she was listening to the quiet as though anticipating the flap of visqueen. Visqueen. She remembered how foolish she'd felt at the Christmas party, not knowing what it was.

She'd been self-conscious from the party's start, aware that the ruffled red dress that looked so cute the week before suddenly seemed little-girlish. The others—men and women from the station—laughed easily, tinkling the ice in their drinks, while Connie nursed an eggnog and wished she knew something to talk to them about.

"Hey, Rick," a balding guy whose name she never did learn yelled across the room. "Did you hear about the documentary I'm going to do? I'm calling it 'The Winter of My Visqueen Tent.'"

Rick laughed. Everyone laughed. Connie even laughed, at everyone laughing, and then asked "What's visqueen?" Everyone laughed some more while Connie stood there, red-faced and feeling stupid. Rick leaned over to her. "It's plastic," he said. Connie wondered if he was as embarrassed to be with her as she was to be there at all.

She apologized when they got home. Rick, lying in bed with his arms folded under his head, had said what a good party it was. "Lots of people never heard of it, Con. It's just a brand name. It's one of those things that makes someone a *real* Alaskan, if they carry a roll of it around in their car or staple some up for a roof. The Fourth Avenue drunks—*they* live in visqueen tents." His smile broke into a laugh, his chest muscles shaking. "What's really funny is that you don't get the joke."

"What's the joke?"

"There's a book—*The Winter of Our Discontent*. It's a pun."

Connie turned out the light before she let herself cry, and when the tears came they were absorbed silently, her face pressed into her pillow.

Just before noon, Connie got ready to drive downtown. As she dressed she kept thinking about the word—*visqueen*. Even the sound of it was unpleasant, like something slimy. Once she knew what it was, she saw it everywhere. It began to seem as much a part of Alaska as the long winter nights and the dirty snow, as the trailer parks and the pickup trucks that coughed dark clouds into the streets.

She was glad to have an excuse to leave the trailer. Without a specific errand, she found it too easy to stay inside until it got dark again. After dark, the car's windshield, smudged with dirt and salt, reflected oncoming lights in a way that blinded her, and she wouldn't go out unless Rick drove.

The tie Rick wanted her to buy had big snowflakes on it—big enough, he said, for the audience to see without a camera zoom. Driving from stoplight to stoplight, dodging potholes, Connie thought Rick was funny—the way he liked to wear something to match his weather forecasts. From a start with a sunny face tie tack, he'd gone on to wear a ski hat when there was a chance of snow, a scarf and ear muffs when it was particularly cold. He had a couple of Hawaiian shirts he wore during balmy spells, and he'd once clumped around the studio with a pair of snowshoes tied to his feet.

Connie parked and climbed over a frozen ridge of gray snow to put her money in the meter. The sidewalk, spread with rock salt, was still scabby with mounds of hard snow and patches of ice. She watched her step carefully, so she didn't see the fur hat until she'd nearly stepped on it.

It was just lying there, the tipped edges of the fur fluffed out, as though it might be some kind of animal curled up asleep. Connie stopped. Ahead of her, a bare-headed old man shuffled away. He looked like one of the Native winos she had become accustomed to seeing hanging around in front of the bars and pawnshops. They were the ones who lived, instead of in the igloos she'd naively expected, in visqueen shelters along the railroad tracks.

She grabbed up the hat and stepped toward him. "Sir," she said. "I think you dropped your hat." When he didn't turn, she felt slightly ridiculous, waving the hat before her, with people watching. Still, she couldn't put it back down, and it was such a nice hat—it would be a shame for him to lose it. She hurried up behind him and nudged him in the shoulder. "Your hat. I think you dropped your hat, sir."

The man turned then, his thick face close to hers, exploding with anger. He shouted something, something so slurred she couldn't make out the words, and reached into his tattered coat sleeve to pull out another fur hat that he shook at her. Stringy gray hair fell across dark, unfocused eyes, and he kept shouting, spit flying from his mouth. Connie couldn't even tell if the words were English.

She backed away, fearful and aware that people were moving past. "Okay," she yelled. "Okay, okay, I'm sorry, forget it, never mind. I'm sorry I bothered you." She flung the hat over a parking meter, then backed away farther, her gloved hands held up empty before her. "Never mind," she said. "I'll leave it right there." Trembling, she moved back along the sidewalk toward the corner. She watched the old man stagger away, dragging one stiff leg. His shoes were no more than street shoes, black and worn down at the heels.

People, still moving past, were looking at her. Connie noticed the smiles. At first they seemed sympathetic, but then she thought she saw a bit of smirk behind them. What a dumb girl, trying to talk to a drunk. Then they were all by–everyone who had watched–and she stepped along past the meter with the hat and entered the store.

Inside, she found that the tie came in half a dozen different colors. Rick hadn't said anything about color. Her hands were still shaking as she fingered the warm silky fabric and held up first one tie and then another. She kept seeing the leathery twisted face of the old man. Surely, when he was younger, he had lived in a village where the men still hunted and the women sewed furs. With only his hat as a link to those times, he stumped in low black shoes and an old army jacket through the dirty, crowded streets of Anchorage. In those same streets, similar hats could end up hanging from parking meters. Studying the ties, she saw them begin to blur. Quickly, she chose the dark green one–the color of thick forests. The snowflakes looked like they could be settling onto needled boughs.

When she walked back to her car, the sky was the same overcast gray and the hat was still parked on the meter. Instead of heading home, Connie drove out to the station and left the tie for Rick. He was in a staff meeting so she didn't get to see him, but she didn't know what she would have told him about the old man anyway. "That's no big deal, Con," he would have said. "Alaska's full of drunks and perverts."

Connie watched the local news while she fixed dinner. Rick liked her to watch the news on his channel so she could tell him how the team looked and whether his part of the show was lively and entertaining. Sometimes she watched one of the other channels so she could tell him when they muffed their lines or got the graphics crooked.

Tonight she had trouble paying attention. There was something about the theft of some walrus tusks and a house fire that killed two cats. Marilyn, the newswoman, looked sufficiently concerned throughout. Then it was sports, and Connie didn't pay any attention at all. She hated most sports, and she didn't much care for the sportscaster Andy, who had asked her at the Christmas party whether she'd ever been a cheerleader.

Then it was Rick, with the weather. He was wearing his yellow sweater over a white shirt and looked handsome. He stood in front of the satellite photo and pointed out the temperatures around the state. It was a generalized pointing, not very precise, and Connie knew that was because Rick couldn't see what he was pointing at. They did something weird with the map—superimposed it or something—so that Rick wasn't actually standing in front of it the way it looked. Then that map was replaced with one of the Lower Forty-Eight, and Rick made more vague hand motions as he, again, didn't see what he was pointing out. There's still a cold spell through the Midwest, he said. Four degrees for Chicago. He held up his hand with four fingers for emphasis.

There was a commercial, and then Rick was back with the forecast. As the camera opened up on him, he was grinning and knotting his snowflake tie. He patted the finished tie against his chest, leaving it on the outside of his sweater. "Guess what, folks," he said, smiling and pointing at his tie. "That's right, the forecast is—Snow!" The camera cut to a photo of some mailboxes with snow crusted over them. The forecast was written over the picture, and Rick read through it. The wind was picking up, pushing the weather front through. Snow would be falling over Anchorage throughout the evening and night. In some parts of town it had already started. Six to eight inches of snow was expected by morning. "So there, all you skiers," Rick said. "This one's for you."

Connie turned the set off and drew back the curtains behind the couch. She knelt on the couch and cupped her hands around her eyes to look out. It was true. Everywhere, within the glow of every light, snow was falling. Already it had taken over, covering the soot, the trash, the gray icy spots. It lay over the trailer court like a clean flannel sheet, softening all the hard edges.

She walked through the trailer, turning off lights. When it was dark within, she lay back on the couch so she could look up into the descending snow. It was thicker now, swirling down like great clumps of pillow feathers. The old Native man, with his hat up his

sleeve, his bare head fleeced white—where would he be? Connie imagined him stumbling in snow-filled shoes toward a visqueen tent.
She saw snow collecting in a dip of the plastic, weighting the tent,
silently dragging the sides down until they collapsed over the sleeping man.

Connie—as though she were as displaced, as alone—could feel the
snow settling over her own face, covering her eyes, filling in the crev-
ices of her nose and mouth, drifting across her entire life. She rolled
from the couch onto her feet, shaking away the sense of suffocation,
and walked to the door. She opened it, and snow blew in, landing on
the front of her sweater, around her feet. Across the way, the visqueen fluttered. The wind moaned along the edge of the trailer,
tossed papers from the counter behind her. Connie knew it was
cold, and that the wind made it even colder. Still, she stood in the
open doorway, listening to the wind drive the weather through the
court, across the country. She felt her own inertia giving way.

Imitations

My hostess has thought of a way to break the ice. "Her dog does imitations," she says, and then, to me, "Why don't you bring him in for a few minutes?"

Tetzel is happy to perform. Grinning, he pulls me into the room. I slow him down with a finger under his collar, sunk into his deep wool. His tail, as long again as his lean black body, sweeps from side to side. I follow it with my free hand, poised to intercept it at the edge of a coffee table covered with hors d'oeuvres and glasses.

We warm up with easy ones. I straighten his ears so they stand upright. Once they're standing I need give them only the barest bracing from behind, my fingers like a couple of wires that stick up behind a Christmas angel to hold a halo in place. After all, he can sometimes stand them up all by himself. It's easiest for him when he's facing into the wind.

"Police dog," I announce.

Everyone—most everyone, unless they're holding drinks—claps. A few people are still talking together. I think I hear someone say "Killer dog," but it's not very loud and I may have misunderstood.

I square myself behind him to hold his head steady while I reach for the corners of his mouth. "Police dog at work," I say, drawing his lips back to reveal fangs, side teeth like old ivory, those black gums with the loose border that always reminds me of the disintegrating, rubberized seal along the edge of my back door. His ears hold their positions, and it's a good snarl-face.

"Thank you, thank you." With a slight curtsy, I acknowledge the applause for both of us.

We move quickly through a couple more. He doesn't care for Pekinese because it involves pushing up his nose and slanting his eyes. He gets to wear my sunglasses for Movie Star. I'm not happy with the name—it's so generic. I'm toying with either Dustin Hoffman, because the nose is close, or Eddie Murphy, because he's black.

The next one's for the literati. There's one place—high on Tetzel's hip, just below where his back leads into the ham—that's like a key in a crank-up toy. Rub it, and he'll flop over in a scratching frenzy, his back leg whup-whup-whupping away in high gear. When he does this, he sits in the most awkward position, with his legs splayed at odd angles and his head leaning off to one side. He gets a real goofy look on his face; his mouth hangs open, his eyes space-out, and his ears bend in opposite directions. If you ever read *The New Yorker*, you know there's a cartoonist in there who draws dogs just like that. "Booth dog," I say. No one gets it. I must be the only person in Alaska who reads *The New Yorker*.

We're losing a few, people who are moving back toward the potato chips, talking instead of watching. "Here's a good one," I say, as soon as Tetzel's done scratching and I can get him to sit up with a more noble look. I turn his ears inside out and fold them back so they sit on top of his head with the sharp pink ridges showing through the fur, the ends touching together on the back of his head. It looks like a hair style. I think the resemblance is truly remarkable, with just that simple folding of his ears. He's already sufficiently hard-eyed and jowly. I start laughing, so hard I can't talk.

Someone makes a guess. "A cat."

I shake my head no.

"My Uncle George."

I choke out, "A head of state."

"The Ayatollah."

I look to see who has said this. It's Larry. He's standing in the kitchen, leaning against the refrigerator. He's looking at me, face like a smart aleck, instead of watching Tetzel.

"Khadafy," he says.

"Margaret Thatcher," I say, and then I return Tetzel's ears to their proper positions.

I've stopped laughing.

At night I wake to the rustle and crunch of his cedar-filled bed. Tetzel stirs, stretches, circles before settling down nose to tail. Dreaming, he kicks against the wall, choking on sharp intakes of breath, like sobs. He is never, like other dogs, the hero of his dreams – the one chasing the cat, the bicycle, or the bitch in heat. Always, he's fleeing, trying to get away. "It's okay, Tetzel. It's okay," I call, soothingly, from my bed, until he stops whimpering. As I fall back to sleep, I'm aware that I match my breathing to his.

Larry pretends to be afraid of him. He does this just to annoy me. "He was going for my throat," Larry says, holding his hands protectively across his neck.

"He was just telling me someone was at the door," I say. I mean, that's what a dog's for. Right? You want him to bark when someone comes to the door.

"He wanted to come *through* the door," Larry says. He's still holding his hands over his throat. "He wanted to eat me for dessert. He wanted to *drink my blood*." He says these last with a Transylvanian vampire's accent.

"He was wagging his tail," I say. "He was happy to see you."

"That's what I mean. He was going to have me instead of kibbles for his TV snack. Don't tell me he doesn't bite."

I don't tell him that, although he knows he doesn't. He *grips*. There's a large distinction. Somewhere in Tetzel's lineage there's an Australian shepherd. That's a sheepherding dog. They're bred to chase along after herds of sheep, nipping at the stragglers and steering the leaders with some directional nudging. I saw pictures in a magazine once. They grab the sheep with their mouths and give a little squeeze. *Gripping:* it's a technical term for the work they do. Pit bulls sink their teeth and hang on, dachshunds dig holes, and dalmations chase after fire trucks. Australian shepherds grip.

He has the raw instinct, but he's never had the practical application or a chance to master the nuances.

I explain it to Larry like this: What if you had never had an opportunity to learn how to swim, but one day you fell into the water? You'd have an instinct to swim, not necessarily a correct, efficient stroke like the crawl, but you'd know how to keep your head above water. You might not even know you were swimming; you'd just do it.

"I'd do the dog paddle," Larry says. "I'd die of hypothermia before I got to shore."

My point is, Tetzel knows he's supposed to grip, but he's not sure what or how hard. He's never seen a sheep in his life. The things he sees going by him while he's lying in the middle of the floor, half-asleep and dreaming about ancestral hard-work times on the range, are people's legs. So he reaches out and *grips*.

Larry swears Tetzel bit him. If you doubt him, he'll roll up his pant leg and point out where the teeth marks were. There's nothing to see, just his hairy white leg. All there ever was were tiny little red spots, like flea bites.

I work at home, so we spend a lot of time together, just the two of us. Tetzel follows me from room to room as I get my breakfast, read the newspaper, answer the phone. When I sit at my desk, doing the bookkeeping my clients bring me, he leans against me. I post expenses, and he plants his paws on my thighs and breathes at me, inches from my face. His breath is offensive; I tell him so. He hikes himself up until he's standing on tiptoe, lying across me like a lap robe, the buffalo kind they used to use in sleighs. He's warm, and his weight puts my legs to sleep. I reach around him to use my calculator.

My house suffers, though not very much. It is a small price.

I know to avoid them, the rough edges around the doorways where Tetzel has removed the trim. He does this when he misses me, when I leave him at home. I have left him when he was sleeping; I thought I'd be back before he awoke. I have closed him in the bedroom, the bathroom, the office, thinking he would think the radio was me, singing in another part of the house. He cannot be fooled.

Larry isn't careful about the doorways. Leaving my bathroom, he snags himself. "Crap," I hear him say. It takes him a minute to disentangle.

"Look at this," he says to me. He's holding the side of his sweater, pointing at a strand of yarn pulled from the knit. "You've got a *nail* sticking out."

"I'm sorry," I say. I would offer to repair the damage if I knew how to knit.

He goes back to the doorway. He opens his knife and prys the nail out. He checks the rest of the doorway, running his hands over the breaks and splinters on either side, from ground level to Tetzel's standing height. He's cursing under his breath, something about trashing. He goes through the other doorway, into the bedroom. He's checking everywhere for hazards.

Tetzel paces the kitchen nervously. He doesn't like swearing.

I give him a Milkbone to cheer him up.

Evenings, we watch television. I watch the screen, and Tetzel lies directly in front of the television, watching me. He doesn't understand that there's a picture behind him. He thinks I'm looking at him, admiring him, being amused by him.

He likes laugh-track comedies and sports programs. He thinks the laughter and applause are for him. I try to share his enthusiasm for basketball.

We start to watch a program about the destruction of the rain forests. Monkeys and birds shriek; Tetzel lifts his head, blocking the screen, concerned. The bulldozers come, grinding against the forest, knocking down trees. I can't help but feel sad and angry. Tetzel's worried; he's afraid I'm finding fault with *him*.

I change the channel, right into the middle of a gunfight. I can't get by it fast enough. Tetzel is on his feet, climbing into my lap, shaking at his close call.

We sit together while a man loses his money in a poker game. It's a sitcom, full of reassuring laughter. Tetzel falls asleep. I smooth the thick fur that surrounds his neck like a cowl.

The phone rings. Tetzel is so far asleep he doesn't even hear it, or he thinks it's part of the television show. I can't reach the phone without waking him. I let it ring.

"You're a *big* boy," I tell him, and he wags his tail. "You're a *good* boy." He wags again. "You're a *good, big* boy.

"You're a *bad* boy," I say in the very same tone of voice. He wags some more.

It's impossible not to love him.

I watch Tetzel sitting outside in the car, leaning back in the driver's seat, turned this way. His eyes are on the front windows here, on the shadows as we walk back and forth through the room—bringing in the food, lighting the candles, raising a toast. He sits erect, still, ears poised to pick up stray sounds from the house.

We eat a turkey, stuffing, mashed potatoes, yams, pumpkin pie. My contribution is the cranberry sauce and a bottle of wine. There are eight or nine of us at the table.

Someone tells about cutting firewood. Someone else says his neighbor had a stackfire. Winter plans are discussed. Several people are going to Hawaii. "What about you?" someone asks me.

"I'm staying here," I say. "I like the winter."

"The winter must be your busy season," she says, "for accounting and taxes and all. It must be hard to get away."

I nod.

"Besides, your dog," someone else says.

"Yes."

We clear the dishes, pour more wine, and divide into teams for Trivial Pursuit. All the answers seem to be Paris or Peter Pan. I excuse myself. "I'll be right back," I say. I don't want them to think I'm leaving.

Tetzel's anxious to get out. He swallows the scrap of turkey skin whole. I dig his tennis ball out from under the seat and throw it up the road. He tosses his head proudly as he returns with it, his tail high and flowing behind him.

Someone else comes out of the house. It's Larry. I think he's going to walk down to the car and talk to me. I try to remember the name of the town in "Leave It to Beaver." I hear Larry strike a match, and I see him sit on the porch step as he smokes a cigarette. I throw the tennis ball again and again. I pat Tetzel on his head and back as he catches his breath. The ball, soaked with saliva, is spongy, oozing.

When I hear the front door close behind Larry, I rearrange Tetzel's blanket and put him back into the car. I'll see how my team's doing and have a cup of coffee.

We drive down to the beach after a rain. The snow, except for spots, has melted off.

Tetzel runs along the top of the beach, sniffing at everything, lifting his leg a thousand times. He sees a flock of gulls in the distance and tears after them, a flurry of legs and smooth galloping motion. He's faster than the speed of sound; he can't hear me when I call. The birds are much more interesting than anything I might have to say.

They fly away and he comes back.

We play stick. He doesn't like to get wet, so I don't throw it into the water, just toward the surfline. He likes that much "chicken": playing at the edge of the surf, close enough that it might lick his paws. For variety, I throw the stick up the beach, down the beach, over a rocky area, back toward the water. I throw it too far and he stands at the water's edge, watching the waves push it forward, then pull it back. He looks at me.

"Fetch," I yell.

He walks away.

And then he's up the cliff, chasing a raven. It *is* a cliff, a nearly vertical wall rising from the beach. He cuts back and forth, lunging for footholds, sending down a shower of sand and rocks. The raven's gone, arched into the sky like a black paper cutout, and Tetzel's heading straight down, pushing an avalanche before him. His legs are faster than his fall, and they stay under him all the way, carrying him back out onto the beach.

His tongue hangs out the side of his mouth—long and pink, the end turned up like a piece of curled ribbon.

Larry waits until Tetzel's settled down in the corner behind my chair. Then he leans over and knocks on the end table. "Come in," he yells.

Tetzel's in the air instantly, crashing past me, rushing to the door, barking and wagging his tail.

Larry thinks it's very funny. He nearly buckles over laughing.

I get up, show Tetzel that no one's at the door, and lead him by the collar into my office. He's so worked up, it takes several minutes to calm him. I rub the top of his head and behind his ears. Saliva drips from his tongue as he pants.

In the living room, Larry's leafing through a magazine. He looks up and smiles at me. His teeth are very large. I open the front door and point into the darkness.

At first Larry doesn't believe I'm serious. He's still smiling with his mouth open. Then his lips come together in a grin and then that shuts down into a straight line.

"The house is getting cold," I say.

Larry picks up his coat and brushes by me. He stomps down the steps so that the whole house shakes.

We wrestle. We both growl, but neither of us means it. I lie across Tetzel with a knee on either side, bury my face in the fur of his neck, roll him back and forth. He puts his mouth around my arm, using it like a hand, to squeeze and caress. He doesn't bite. He doesn't even grip. He kicks at me with his feet. I fall sideways and tickle his belly. "Soo-ey, soo-ey, soo-ey," I say. It doesn't mean anything; it's just a nonsense word that sounds right to say to him. If it's ridiculous, it's just between him and me.

When we're wrestled-out, I take his two front paws and hold them. The pads are dry and just a tiny bit rough, like the finest grade of sandpaper. My fingers stroke them, reach into the soft fur that lines the spaces like grass in the cracks of a walk. I hold his paws in one hand, and I smooth his face, flattening an ear to the side of his head. I put my head against his. He's got that good dog smell. I breathe it all the way to the bottom of my chest, that warm and musky good smell.

The Bucket of Mice

Dick stretched out in the lawn chair and put his feet up on the buoy. He tilted his head all the way back, draining the glass of iced tea. God, wouldn't Kitty love it here today, he thought for the hundredth time. He had just checked the thermometer, and it was 75 degrees in the shade. He looked down at his bare chest and saw that he was getting burned. Well, he just couldn't help it; the sun was too rare and pleasurable to avoid. He pulled the bill of his Suzuki Outboards cap down a little more, to shade his nose.

Off the end of the dock the water, which had lain as flat as flagstones all day, was getting up a little the way it did at the top of the tide. The rollers hitting the beach advanced the sun's glare rhythmically, the glitter at each crest like the diamonds on a camera lens when a picture was shot into the sun. Dick was reminded of the photography in some old surfing movie – *The Endless Summer,* he thought. Jesus, it was beautiful. An eagle flapped by, low, eyeing the net out front. There were so many eagles this year, they seemed nearly as common as gulls. Dick was torn between being impressed and discrediting them as just another gang of scavengers.

Kitty would like it here today, he thought again. So would the kids. He pictured them at the edge of the surf, in sunsuits, splashing into the water, running back along the sand. He smiled at his vision of their stiff barefooted walk across the rocks, their "ouching" from

the sharp edges as they thrust out brown knees and elbows like mari-
onettes. Well, maybe not sunsuits. That was a few years ago. Now it
would be cutoffs and T-shirts with funny sayings. "Beat it," one of
Kenny's read. It was from some music group. Dick was afraid to ask
him what the "it" was; he wanted to think it was a drum.

Kitty had said, at first, that it was the children who didn't want to
come. "Kenny really wants to be in Litttle League this summer,"
she'd argued. "All his friends are playing. And Niffy wants so badly
to go to the riding camp. And they both need to take swimming
lessons."

Not believing her, he had asked them himself. He was shameless;
he admitted it. He flattered, he cajoled. He bribed. "Kenny, you're
big enough now to earn ten percent as my fishing partner. You don't
even have to save it all for college." And for Niffy, "When we get
back, we can see about *buying* you a horse of your own."

He suspected his desperation showed. They seemed sorry, re-
spectful even, but no, they had whispered, they didn't want to go to
Alaska, to spend another summer on the beach.

It was wrong, probably, to have accused Kitty of turning the
children against him. "Me?" she'd said. "*Me?* Did I offer them
money and a horse?" When she'd laughed she tossed her head, and
he could see the row of fillings in the back of her mouth. "Can't you
understand?" she said. "They've got their own lives. They're not
going to sacrifice them every summer, to do what you want." When
he walked out of the room, she'd said behind him, "That goes for me
too. I've had it with Alaska, and I've had it with you."

I've had it with you.

Dick slapped at a moosefly, and the slap stung his thigh. When he
pressed his skin with his thumb, testing, it left a white mark. He
wondered if he should lie down so that the back of him could cook
instead. Some people did those things. They'd had a neighbor,
when he was a kid, who used a kitchen timer to clock his tan, flipping
over every half hour to keep it even. Dick didn't have that kind of
vanity, though. He simply wanted to go home in August fit and tan,
so that Kitty would be jealous of his summer in the sun. He looked
at his belly, pink but layered in folds because of how he was sitting.
He spread a roll with his fingers. In the crease it was as white as a
beluga whale. Well, there was still time to get fit, too. Fishing didn't
really begin in earnest for another week or so.

He heard the boat's motor. That would be Wally coming back from the point. That kid sure was good with boats; Dick had to give him credit for that. He heard the boat slow, and he knew that Wally had stopped to check the middle net. He hoisted himself out of the chair and opened the cabin door to get the binoculars from their nail. Crossing to the front corner of the dock, he focused on the blue boat in the distance.

Wally, in the bow, was lifting the corkline as he moved his way along it, checking for fish. Dick watched him stop at something dark in the net and work it free, then toss it away. A stick, probably, or maybe a trout, though he thought that Wally would have saved the trout. They hadn't had so many, yet, that they were sick of eating them. Wally reached the end of the net and dropped the corkline back into the water, then started the motor and headed back. He would learn. There wasn't any point in fishing so hard this early in the season. It didn't hurt, though, getting the practice.

Dick poured himself another glass of iced tea, took a swallow, and then regretted having left the pitcher in the sun. It wasn't even real iced tea, because he didn't have any ice; it was just a mix, made with creek water. Ice was one of the things he missed. He would try to remember, when the tender came by to pick up their fish, to ask for a bag of ice.

There weren't many things he missed at the beach. He liked the isolation, the distance from crowds and television laughter. It was basic here – simple – and he liked that. Shelter, sunlight, a tide rolling in and then rolling out again, fox tracks in the sand. What more could a person want, besides his family with him?

They had always spent summers fishing at the beach – he since college days, Kitty since their marriage, the kids since birth. They had even planned both pregnancies so that Kitty conceived early in the summer and the babies were born early enough – February and March – to be big enough to travel to the beach in June. Dick had always thought that the beach was the perfect place for kids, for being a family together. He had always made it a priority, shaping his working life around it. He was lucky his company, from the start, had let him have summers off, though he knew he paid in other ways for the privilege.

Walking back along the dock, Dick found some shade for the pitcher behind a corner of the gear shed. The shed's closed door reminded him about the bucket. That morning, when he'd brought in a salmon the birds had ruined, he'd looked for something to put the eggs in. He'd gone into the shed to get the plastic bucket. When he picked it up, he reached in to flick out what he thought were some dried leaves. Then he'd seen what they were. Dead mice. He'd looked closer. One was curled up in a ball, nose to tail, as though asleep. A second was also curled up, though not so tightly, and it had a gaping hole in its side. And then there was one that was just flat, like a miniature hide that had been tanned, a Tom Thumb rug. Dick had set the bucket back where he found it and went to wash his hands.

It was immediately clear to him, what had happened. The mice had fallen from the shelf under the workbench into the bucket, and then they couldn't get out. The first one, what was now the little rug, got eaten by the next one. Then the third one ate the hole in the second one. Dick had lathered his hands extra well.

Wally, now, was walking up the beach. His hipboots looked heavy and hot. Dick would tell him about turning them down, how it made it easier to walk.

He saw Kitty then, in his mind as in a motion picture, trudging up the beach, a small matte figure against the dazzling sea. Then he saw her, eyes flashing with the same hard sparks, saying "I've had it." He still didn't know if she meant it, the first part or the second, Alaska or him. She hadn't told him, though, that she didn't mean it. He needed to decide whether that was because she'd forgotten that she ever said it, or because it was the truth.

Wally sat at the table, playing solitaire, one game after another. Day after day, hour after hour, he sat and did this, turning the cards, ya-hooing, muttering under his breath, counting out loud, announcing his score, writing it down where he kept a list of his wins and losses. "Watch out, Las Vegas," he said now, shuffling the cards.

It drove Dick nuts, the incessant slapping of cards. When they'd first arrived, Wally had asked him to play, but the only games Wally knew were juvenile—Gin Rummy, War, something called Kings in the Corners. After a couple rounds of each, Dick had begged off.

"I'm not much of a card player," he'd apologized. So Wally played lots of solitaire. Sometimes, Dick observed, he dealt gin rummy hands and played against himself.

Wally was Kitty's cousin. He was young, just twenty, and just out of the Army. Dick wondered how anyone could have lived for twenty years and have learned so little. He kept being surprised, even after five days of nearly constant companionship, at how naive the boy was. Naive was not the right word. Slow, maybe. Stupid. Not a fast learner. Dick had noticed that he didn't read, not even the back of the cereal boxes; everything he knew came from what he'd heard or seen as he'd slid through life. He didn't know what a spatula was, for god's sake. "Would you hand me the spatula?" Dick had asked. "The what?" Dick had got it himself. "Oh, the flipper-thing."

Dick was aware that he had already altered his way of talking to accomodate Wally, acquiescing to the lowest common denominator. His vocabulary was becoming more limited every day, and he feared that eventually he'd be stuck with words as crude as good and bad. "This sure is a good life," he had just heard himself say.

"You like baching it?" Wally asked.

Each time Wally lifted his arms to gather in the cards, as he did now, Dick got a whiff of sour body odor. He decided to become a mouth-breather, to rescue his appetite. "No," he said. He checked the rice; it was still watery.

"I didn't think so. If I was married, my wife would be with me."

Dick ran a hand over his forehead, wondering if it was meant as a put-down. He decided not, that Wally simply wasn't thinking as he stated his expectations. Wally, he had already learned, had an old-fashioned sense of male supremacy. He wondered what pathetic girl would ever marry him, what she'd see in him. She'd probably be a dynamo, he thought, at Crazy Eights.

Wally was Kitty's idea. As soon as Dick had said, "But you have to come, I need you for my fishing partner," she had smiled with the knowledge that it was all figured out. "He needs something to do, Dick," she'd said. "He can't find a job and he's driving his mother crazy. He's a hard worker, and it would be a good experience for him. And you'd be a good influence on him, a positive role model." Dick could tell it was a speech she'd been practicing.

Dick removed the lid from the rice and frowned into the pot, waiting for the water to boil off. He didn't know how he'd last another six
and a half weeks. It just wasn't the same without Kitty and the kids,
with Wally. "Finish up your game there," he said. "Soup's on."

During dinner Dick decided to call Kitty. He told Wally that he
was going to walk up to the neighbors to use their radio-telephone,
but he didn't invite him along. He needed to be by himself to think,
and he especially didn't want Wally hanging around listening to him
talk to Kitty.

As he put on his jacket he said to Wally, "There's a plastic bucket
in the shed that we're going to use. I noticed today that it needs to be
cleaned. It looks like it's got some dried-up old mice in it." He
smiled, to show it was nothing to be squeamish about. "Would you
clean it out while I'm gone, give it a good scrub?"

Wally turned sharply. "Why should I?"

Dick's first thought was, Kenny would never talk back to me like
that. Then, as though Kenny had, he said, reflexively, "Because I
asked you to." Wally stood without moving but Dick could feel him
hesitating, unsure of the challenge. He noticed that Wally was taller
than he'd realized, with well-developed shoulders and no stomach
flab. Wally could beat him hands down in an actual fight. "Well,
because I fixed dinner," he said, "and that seems like an equivalent
kind of chore."

"I was going to do the dishes," Wally said.

"Well, fine." Dick looked at the tidiness he'd left. He'd served on
paper plates so there was only the one pot to wash.

On his way up the beach, Dick thought how stupid it was to have
a confrontation over something like cleaning out a bucket. Still, the
mere thought of having to do it himself upset him. He didn't want
to have to look at the dead mice again, and what if they wouldn't
shake out onto the beach, if he had to scrape at the bits of adherent
fur? And then, at some point, he'd have to put his hand inside to
scrub it.

At the neighbors' Matt helped him place the call, and then he and
Linda and all three of their girls stepped outside so Dick could have
some privacy. Privacy, such as it was. Dick knew people tuned in to
the channel, just for fun. He'd caught Matt's family doing it before,
Saturday nights with popcorn.

Kitty sounded anxious when the operator asked her to accept the charges. She wasn't expecting to hear from him, and he realized that the call probably panicked her. He imagined the series of potential disasters that would flash through her head before he even got to speak.

"Dick," she said, "is everything all right?"

"Everything's fine," he rushed to tell her. "I just wanted to call you. How's everything there?"

"Good," she said. "We're all fine. The kids are asleep. Should I wake them? Do you want to talk to them?"

"No." He scratched at his jaw; his new beard was still like a stiff brush, the kind he imagined floors were polished with. "I just wanted to check and see how things were going. How's Little League?"

"They're three and one right now. Kenny's been batting very well." She went on, telling him about the previous day's game. There wasn't a hint of being sorry, of any doubt that baseball could be inferior to life at the beach. "His fielding needs more work," she said.

Dick wondered if she knew what she'd said, and how it might have sounded to him. Or had she meant to strike at him like that, criticizing his absence? A *good* father would be there, playing catch in the backyard. He pictured Kenny alone in the yard, like a child of divorce, tossing a ball up and down. "And Niffy," he asked, when they'd exhausted baseball. "How's camp?"

"She loves it. She's crazy about the horses. That's all she talks about."

"Yourself?"

"Just fine." Her voice had a lilt to it, a pleasantness that didn't sound completely natural. Actually, Dick realized, she sounded like she did when she talked to her mother on the phone—sweetsy-talk, just the straight, not-to-worry news, regardless of whatever was really going on. "You know I got that bid to landscape the new bank," she was saying. "That's mostly what I'm doing, between carting the kids around to their activities. I like it, being outdoors, moving dirt around and making things grow."

"The weather's been beautiful here," he told her. "I'm sunburned."

She laughed. "You're trying to make me jealous. It won't work. How's fishing?"

"Slow. You know how it is this early."

"How's Wally working out?"

"Okay. He's good with the boat, except that he likes to burn up too much gas."

"He always was good with motors and things."

Dick didn't want to spend money to talk about Wally. He tried to think of something else. "Guess what I saw just now, walking up to use the phone?"

"What?"

"A fireweed blossom."

"Oh, fireweed," she said, with the first suggestion of longing. "You knew I'd miss the fireweed. It's still my favorite flower."

Dick was confused, then annoyed. He hadn't known that fireweed was her favorite. That wasn't why he'd mentioned it. Had she forgotten the significance? "Actually," he said, "what I meant was about the timing of the fish. You know the old rule of thumb—when the fireweed blooms, that's when the sockeye hit the beach."

"Is that right? I guess I'd forgotten. Well, I hope your nets get so plugged with fish that you can barely lift them into the boat." Her voice sounded so far away, thousands of miles away, and as though she had no idea what she was talking about. It also sounded like the end of a conversation, the well-wished remark that a person saved for last, after which there remained nothing more to say.

"Well, good-bye then," he said.

As he cleared the call he realized that she *was* thousands of miles away. Three thousand, anyway. He also realized that he hadn't said any of the things he'd meant to: I love you, I miss you, I wish you were here. But she hadn't said anything that he wanted to hear, either: I love you, I miss you, I didn't mean what I said before. Sure, there were people listening, but they could have said those things. He was tempted to call back, but somebody else had already put a call through. Reluctantly, while the caller read a long list of groceries, Dick hung up the microphone. After "chocolate chips," he turned off the set. It was more than he could stand, the idea of someone baking cookies.

On the way home, he reconstructed the conversation, noting the places where it should have gone differently. He was sorry he hadn't thought about it more before calling. He was sorry that he'd called at all, he decided. He kicked a stick of driftwood out of the way. His loose shoe had filled with sand, but he didn't stop to empty it or lace it up. He wondered if Kitty had a lover. He had never questioned her faithfulness before, not once in all their years together. Would she do that? He pictured a man in the room with her, smoking a cigarette while she talked so guardedly on the phone.

The image was too painful. Dick stopped and stared at the sea, blocking his vision with its solid, blue-gray mass. The lick of water on the shore was barely audible, like a kitten's tongue on milk. She wouldn't do that. Even if she wanted to, she wouldn't, because of the kids. Kids noticed things. She'd be afraid they'd tell him. And he remembered that she'd asked if he wanted her to wake them. She wouldn't have if someone was with her. Dick felt better, but still, this was something he hadn't considered before, and he didn't like it. He thought of the bankers leering from their windows while Kitty, in shorts and a halter top, shoveled their topsoil.

Back at camp, he nearly tripped over the plastic bucket. It sat, overturned, on the dock at the top of the stairs. Dick hesitated, then gripped the handle between finger and thumb and lifted so that the bucket swung upright. Inside, it was as clean as if it had just come from the hardware store. He smiled sheepishly and set it to one side.

When he opened the door, Wally got up from the table where he'd been playing cards and, awkwardly, carried a pot from the counter to the table. "I made some dessert," he said. He turned to get bowls and spoons, and Dick looked into the pot. Butterscotch pudding. He wondered if Wally knew it was his favorite flavor.

"Thanks," Dick said, sitting down. "That's very thoughtful." He smoothed his serving with the back of his spoon. "Thanks," he said, "for cleaning the bucket."

"Sure," Wally said.

Wally got a damp sponge and wiped a pudding drip from the table. "Multi-purpose sponge," he said.

"Huh?"

Wally held up the sponge, smeared with the pudding. "First it cleans the dishes, then the bucket, then the table."

Dick got up quickly, the pudding in his stomach trying to overtake him on the way. He fought to keep it down.

"Just kidding," Wally laughed. "I thought you'd like that."

Dick sat down and rested before he could pick up his spoon again. Really, goddamn dead mice. You'd think it was a big thing. Wally turned on the radio but kept it low. Dick had already let him know what he thought about loud rock music. Listening to the music—it was hardly rock at all, more acoustical and with a flute solo—Dick suddenly felt the warm glow of guilt-induced tolerance. "You know, you're all right, Wally," he said.

Wally looked at him doubtfully. "You mean that?"

"Of course I mean it. Why wouldn't I mean it?"

"Well, you never say anything. I've been trying real hard, but you never say anything. I thought maybe I was fucking up." He paused, then he asked, "Did you call home?"

Dick remembered that he'd been in the Army. It sounded like something Army boys would ask each other. "Yes."

"How're the wife and kids? Everything okay?"

"Fine," Dick said. "Kitty sends her best."

"Tell her I say 'hi' next time you talk to her. Tell her we miss having a woman around the place."

The way Wally said it, Dick had the feeling he meant having some-one around to handle the cleaning chores, like the bucket of mice. Kitty would have taken care of that the first day, without a com-ment. Again he pictured the mice, the three stages of disembodi-ment. Even with the other two to eat, and even though there was some of the middle mouse left, the last mouse still died. He won-dered what it was—dehydration, cold, loneliness, shame, or some worse suffering he couldn't begin to imagine. He saw that Wally was waiting, patiently, for him to respond. How could he say how he missed her and how much he feared losing her, any more than he could admit to being disturbed by the sight of dead and eviscerated mice?

"Yeah," he said. He said it quickly, a word as final as a period or as Kitty's hope for fish as she'd signed him off, a word so final that even Wally had to know the conversation was over.

Waiting for the Thaw

Ben wriggles around, crowding closer. He's cold. More than that, he wants his mother to be awake. He presses against her, feeling for her heartbeat. It's not a beat he can count, separate knocks through her skin. It's more a constant soft rustle, like a mouse scratching around under a pile of dry leaves. There's so much cloth between them—her heavy nightgown, his sweater over a shirt over an undershirt—he finds it hard to draw any heat or to feel her rhythm against his own.

He lifts himself to his knees and leans over so he can see his mother's face. Her eyes are closed. He breathes against her face; the wisps along her hairline flutter. He blows a little harder, bearing down on the hairs like a wind that lays the grasses flat.

When she opens her eyes she frowns, focusing on his face. Her eyes are ringed with puffed ridges that descend to wrinkles like rain gullies, but the irises are a clean, clear wash of green. "Cut it out," she says, her voice just above a whisper. She rolls away from him, pulling the covers with her, wrapping them tightly across her shoulders.

Ben rolls over, too. He stares off the edge of the bed. His father's moccasins are on the floor, pointing at each other. One is upright, the way it should be, but the other is flipped over. The bottom leather looks like his father's foot: big toe, smaller toes, heel. The leather's worn thin and baggy and shiny-black, a print of his father's bare foot like the track an animal leaves in the snow.

Rise and shine. It's a new day dawnin'. We got places to go and things to do, coffee to brew. I got a trapline to tend to. You, too, Ben. No son of mine's gonna be a slug-a-bed. I see you watchin' me. You're like a little rabbit, crouched under a branch, just watchin' me and listenin' with your ears all atwitter.

"Mama," he says. "It's cold again."

Ben waits, knowing she won't answer. He looks out from the bed, his eyes level with the desk cluttered with papers and catalogs, and tries to determine how cold it is. It's not so bad, under the blankets and comforter, but his nose, sticking out, feels dry like bone. He hasn't heard the stove crackle in a long time.

He tries to remember the last time he was up. The window was paler then, its edges fuzzy within the blackened walls. He used the flashlight to reach the other room, setting it down like a spotlight while he peed into the can. She got up, too, before or after that; he remembers hearing her own rattle in the can. He heard the stove door swing open and shut, her heaved sighs of weariness as she dropped the logs inside. It was pitch-dark then, but he saw the circle of light darting over the walls as she came back toward the bed, heard the click as it went out and her sighs again, then felt her stiff curled form ease into dream. He dreamed, too—long, vivid dreams filled with animals and strange places, the kind of dreams that come only after sleeping to the point of exhaustion.

I know you don't like the dark. So use more gas. It's worth it. Light more lanterns and burn them longer. I'll be back quick as I can—three days if I move fast. Keep busy—you got plenty to do. Just make sure you get up in the morning. Set the damn clock so you do it.

It's daylight now, the log walls rising dimly around them to the ceiling, boxing them in evenly. Ben closes his eyes and pretends it's another morning, his father at home. He likes waking in his own bed when it's still dark, hearing voices, the squeak of the stove. The smell of coffee comes next, then meat frying. When he opens his eyes, his mother will be looking down at him, her hair shiny, parted, pulled around her head with silver clips. Her hands will be white with flour, busy.

He turns his head into the covers and sucks at the imagined scent of hot bread, but it's the sour smell of unwashed clothes he breathes. His empty stomach nags him. He rolls onto it, thinking to press out the pinch, but it doesn't help. He rolls back. He kicks against his mother's legs. "Get up," he urges. "Get up."

She says something into her pillow. He climbs over her to hear her say it again. "I can't," she says. "I just can't do it, baby." She's crying again, tears sliding down the side of her nose like rain down the crease of a leaf.

Ben crawls from beneath the covers and pads to the stove. He pushes on the handle and swings the door free. At its squeak, he looks back at the bed, but his mother doesn't move. There's still fire inside, embers as red as eyes at night: a fox frozen in a flashlight beam. Ben takes a piece of kindling and lays it over the coals. He goes to a woodpile just inside the door and cradles a log into his arms, clasping it to his chest. Back at the stove, he releases it into the fire with a crash and a cloud of ash. He returns to the pile for another. When he closes the stove door he can hear the kindling catching. It's a friendly sound, like talk. He brushes pieces of bark from his sweater.

I got a fire goin' for you. No excuse now. Wake it and shake it, wag it and shag it, if you can't carry it throw it out and drag it.

In the kitchen, he gets a pilot cracker from the box and spreads it with peanut butter. There's something more he wants, some other taste to fill the hollow, something hot. He looks at the row of cans and jars along the top of the counter. He knows what they are—beans, rice, popcorn, macaroni—but they're all hard, raw. He opens a coffee can of sugar and sticks a wet finger in. He sucks his finger and dips it in again. He puts the lid back on and reaches for a jar of raisins. They're sweet, too, and he chews a mouthful, but it's not sweetness he wants. He lifts the lid on a can of Tang and puts some in a cup, then dips water from the barrel. "Tang," he says to the can, tracing out the large white letters. The picture, of a pitcher and a glass of juice, looks much better than what he has. He stirs his cup with a spoon, around and around, until the waves break over the side, slopping to the counter. Carefully, he wipes it up with a sponge.

I know you don't like bein' left alone. You're not alone. Ben's good company. He's gettin' smarter every day. Find me another five-year-old who talks as good as he can, when he's got somethin' to say. Talk to the trees. I do. I talk to everything. Go outside and talk to the world. You should get out more, anyway. Anyone would get cabin fever stayin' indoors all the time.

Ben climbs down from the chair and skates over the floor to two of his trucks. With one in each hand, he scoots along on his knees, growling motor noises. He drives the dump truck into a crack, tipping it to one side and then the other. The pickup spins in a circle and runs into the side of the bigger truck. "Ka-boom," he says. He looks through the wide doorway at the heap of bedclothes. He straightens out the trucks again and rolls them, first one leading and then the other, through the doorway to the space in front of the stove. In the arc of warmth, he sets up a course—along the edge of the hearth, through the tunnel of an open magazine, around a slipper, along a twisty trail of string. "R-r-r-oom," he says quietly. "A-roo-a-roo," like his father's snowmachine coming down the river, gunning up the last hill, popping over the bank into the yard.

Finally Ben stretches out on the floor, his head on one arm. He rolls the smaller truck back and forth in the same spot, listening to the whir of its wheels. It's so warm, he feels like one of the lynx his father tosses behind the stove to thaw. Curled up tightly at first, the cats loosen as they soften, melting into friendliness. When the cold goes out of them, he likes to play with the heavy paws, tickling the pads, feeling for the retracted claws. He likes to bend the ankles and the knee joints back and forth, pretending to make them run. Get your face out of that poison, his mother says when he lays a cheek against the fur. He can smell it, too close—the spray his father uses to kill fleas before he brings the cats inside.

With his head on the floor, he watches the bed. Sideways, there's still nothing moving. He imagines the lynx, thawed now, hanging by a foot from the nail in the beam. Sideways like this, the cat would look stretched out, running. It's his father, sitting at the end of the bed, the covers pushed back behind him, who would be turned the wrong way. His father–in the glow of a lantern, cutting around the toes, peeling fur down a leg, exposing red muscle–would work slowly, skillfully, to skin the cat. Turning it inside out, he'd make one animal into two–the hollowed-out thick wrap of fur and the skinny, red-raw, sinewy other. Ben is always surprised to see them together, apart, the one stripped from the other, the other gutted from the one. He closes his eyes, wishing that when he opens them his father will be there, at the end of the bed, peeling back a leg, the sound like sticky tape pulling off paper.

This is the life, ain't it? It's a sin a person can have it so good, walkin' around in the woods all day long, just listenin' and lookin' at God's earth the way he made it, not all messed up the way it is everywhere else. Doin' a little pre-datorin'–just part of Nature's chain. Right, Ben? You watch how I do this. You'll be havin' your own traps before long. You can start with them snares I tried to get your mother to do.

There's a noise, like a feeble wind blowing through. Ben opens his eyes but doesn't move. He waits to hear if it'll come again. An arm scratches under the covers, then comes free over the top.

Ben slips over to the bed to watch his mother. Her arm lies as she flung it, palm up, the fingers gently cupped as though around a ball of yarn. The wrist above her sleeve is narrow and white, raised with blue veins like braids of a river. Her pulse twitches along the ridge of bone. Ben looks at her face. The side on which she's lying is pushed up, folding a smooth cheek into her nose. Her eyelashes lie thickly snagged. After a while her eyes open. Ben can see the square of window reflected in the green shallows.

"Baby," she says.

Ben pulls himself up to sit against her.

"I was dreaming," she says. She sighs. "It was sunny. I was eating something like pineapple, the juice was trickling down my chin, making me sticky. I think it was Hawaii." Her glance pulls away from Ben and traces over the dark walls, coming to rest at the window. Her eyes squint shut.

Ben nudges her, desperate not to lose her again. "Let's have cocoa," he says. "Let's make hot cocoa."

Her eyes stay shut, squeezed at the edges as though she's trying to bring the other place back. "In a little bit, baby. Maybe in a little bit."

When Ben tires of watching her, he slides off the bed and gathers some magazines from the desk, then climbs back onto the bed. Turning pages, he looks at pictures of people at a fair, staring at a pig and eating, of a white church surrounded by trees with red and orange leaves, and of a vegetable stand with pumpkins, more colored leaves around it. In the other it's mostly food pictures; Ben lingers over one that shows a ham crisscrossed and studded with cloves, with a pot of creamed corn steaming beside it. There are pictures of clothes, too—ladies' clothes. They show mostly skin—bare arms instead of sleeves, necklines laid open, lengths of thin legs. He thinks of his mother in wool trousers and bunny boots, buried beneath sweaters and parkas, hats and scarves. No one in magazines looks like that. He turns back to the first one. The women at the fair wear print dresses with waists, and sandals.

There's the other difference, too. He flips through both magazines together, side by side. They're all smiling—all the women—or, at the least, looking interested. His mother doesn't often look like that. He remembers each time that she does. He's seen it when she invites canoers to stop for coffee. He's seen it when, meeting a plane, she rips open a letter with her teeth and reads it, the paper fluttering in her mittened clutch. It's when they go to town—the rare trips to the dentist and to buy supplies—that he's seen it most. She's so different—rushing around, driving a car, going to stores, talking to people, calling on the telephone. He doesn't know her then; she seems lighter, as though she's come out from under the weight of her winter parka. He holds on to her, afraid she might disappear into the crowd on a street, like a duck that would fly off to join a flock.

Ben goes back into the kitchen and pees into the can, then finishes the cracker. He climbs into his snowsuit, zipping carefully, and forces his feet into his shoepacs. He tightens the laces the way his father showed him, working from the bottom; he does everything except tie them. Then he pulls on his hat and mittens. As he opens the door, parting the strips of fur around its edges, a cloud of condensation billows in. Ben shuffles through, tugging the door closed behind him.

He can tell it's cold by how quickly the mucus in his nose freezes into plugs like a couple of dry beans. When he looks up, blinking, his eyes feel as though they're lined with crisp white paper. The sun slouches somewhere below the line of spruce that tops the bank across the river; this time of winter there are just two gaps where the sun slips through on its low traverse. With the overcast, the sky's the same flat white as the land, as though it could flip either way and be the same sandwich.

Except for the squeak of his feet on the dry snow and the slippery sound his breath makes against the nylon of his snowsuit, Ben doesn't hear anything as he walks to the bank. At the edge he strains his ears, hoping to hear the distant mosquito-like buzz of the snow-machine. There's nothing. The cold and the silence match exactly, as though sound itself is frozen. The river's flow lies buried beneath deadening layers of snow and ice. There's no wind; the hoarfrost thickens the trees, feathering every twig like mold. It's too cold even for birds; even the camp robbers who usually flap around the yard are gone.

Your ma, she never took to the cold the way I did. It's so peaceful is why I like it. It's kind of like everything stops.

Summers, it's never so quiet. The river runs, rolling over itself, slapping at the rocks and along the shoreline, whispering its way by. Birds call; ravens' wings rustle as they lift overhead. Wind combs the trees with a hum of needles and a click of leaves. At night, from back up the river, come the voices of wolves, the high-pitched beggaring of the pups.

With freeze-up, all that ends. The only sounds Ben can think of— the snowmachine, the chainsaw, the scrunch of boot on snow, his father's words muffled behind a face stiff with frost—all seem un-natural, imposed, short-lived.

He walks back toward the cabin, stopping to look at the martens. They lie in a heap, frozen into contorted positions. Ben thinks they look like circus animals, twisted in the shapes of tricks, with fancy fur cuffs at their ankles like costumes. Skinned, blood-red, their faces are pinched, their bodies long and gaunt, their tails like pencils sharpened to points.

Ben likes the marten bodies, especially when they're still warm, when he can make them run on the cabin floor, make them dance to the music on the radio. He likes to wag their tails. Now, his hands thrust deep into his pockets, he only wants to look. With their wet shine gone dull as hammered iron, he knows that touching them with bare hands would hurt.

"You got more of you coming. All of you will be all together. Visitin' together, too, 'cept your mouths froze." The sound of his voice plunges into the air and is gone, as though he'd spit and seen his spit sink like a pellet into the snow.

Ben walks in a slow circle. He passes the cache where the frozen hunks of moosemeat hang. The camp robbers were here before, pulling at the burlap; the ground is littered with specks of meat and a scattering of long stiff hairs. He passes the mountain of firewood, remembering his father swinging the axe, one crack to each split, moving through the stack of logs in smooth easy motions – bend, straighten, swing, toss the pieces to the top of the hill.

At first the sound is so faint he thinks he's imagining his father stepping around the woodpile to grab another log. He pushes at his hat to lift it from his ears. It's true – someone's walking. He can hear the squeak of one foot, then the other, a steady advance. His father wouldn't be walking, though. His father has the snowmachine. Ben looks around quickly to see if his mother might have come from the cabin. He looks back, trying to locate the sound. It seems to fall from the air, dropping out of the trees like snow weighted and slicked by a thaw. But it's louder, and then his eyes settle on the woods ahead where the trail that winds along the river opens out.

He sees the movement first, flashing between trees, then the dark shape of his father's snowmachine suit. There he is, walking from the woods, huge and fat in all his bulk, his mittened hands propelling him forward. He's not wearing his mask, and his red face is ringed with frost that coats his beard and the ends of his hair.

"Ben! Jeez. I nearly didn't see you standin' there so quiet." His father spreads his arms and Ben flies into them, hugging himself to the rough cloth. The stiff beard showers snow as he brushes against it.

"Wouldn't you know? I went and ran out of gas about three miles short. Don't I feel like a fool." He lifts Ben and carries him toward the cabin. "After we get some chow, maybe you'll walk back with me. I got a whole sledload of furs. Even a wolverine. Man, they are the ugliest animals. Wait 'til you see this one. His face is froze just as ugly as he is."

His father sets Ben down by the door. "You comin' in?" he asks. "If you wait, I'll be right back with the saw to cut some steaks. I don't suppose your mother's got anything thawed out and ready to go." Ben inspects the plastic sled leaning next to the step. His father stamps his feet and goes inside.

Ben waits, listening. The door is too thick, the walls too solid to leak any of the talk. In a few minutes, his father reappears with the saw, and Ben follows him to the meat. After lowering one of the pieces, his father lays it on a sawbuck and yanks the saw back and forth across its end. Ben stands close, watching the pale dust fall onto the snow.

Halfway through, his father stops to rest. "Your mother," he says, squinting toward the river, then looking down at Ben, "did she feed you at all?"

Ben thinks of his mother in bed, waking to tell him about pineapples and sunshine. He looks back down at the meat dust.

His father sighs. He begins to saw again, quick strokes grinding through with a rhythmic, two-tone whine. When he's done he hands the fur-rimmed slab to Ben, rewraps the meat, and hoists it back to its place. "C'mon," he says, twisting Ben's hat around on his head. "Let's eat."

Ben's mother is at the cookstove, feeding the fire and heating a pot of coffee that's just starting to cheer the room with its smell. She's dressed, with her hair brushed back out of her eyes. Ben hands her the steak, and she lays it on a board to trim off the hide and fat. Ben's father takes the bucket of urine from the corner of the room and carries it outside. No one says anything.

When the meat's ready—and the potatoes and the canned corn—they sit and eat together. Ben's father tells about the wolverine's ugly face, about the thirty-seven martens and the thickness of their cold-weather furs, about the cabin at the end of the line that squirrels got into, and about the cubbies that worked best and the way he carefully reset them with a scatter of snow and a sweep of bough. Ben's mother sits behind her cup of tea, nodding, her eyes as shiny as melting ice.

"Well." Ben's father stands and stretches. "Ben and me are gonna take a can of gas and fetch my loot home before it gets too dark."

"No." Ben's mother says it quietly, stiffening. Her shoulders pull up around her.

"I was gonna say," his father adds, "why don't you come with us? It'll be a nice walk. Just an hour or so, and then we can all ride back. It'll do you good to get out."

"No. I'm not and he's not. I don't want to be alone."

"*You* don't want to be alone! What do you think *he's* been, here with you?"

Ben looks into his plate, at the swirls and patterns of solidifying grease. He knows the shine of his mother's eyes has overflowed into tears that fall down her face. He listens as his father crosses to her and wraps his arms around her from behind. "He's coming," he says softly into her hair, "and I'd like it if you would too."

Nobody moves. Staring at his plate, Ben feels his mother gradually yield to his father's embrace. "Go," she says. "The two of you go, and I'll clean up here. I want to clean up while it's light."

His mother helps him with his boots and ties a scarf around his face. He can barely see through the slot she leaves him. She's turned away, pouring herself another cup of tea, when they leave the cabin.

Ben clutches his father's thick hand. He thinks about the wolverine, eager to stroke its black cape, to see its face set in anger, to draw its claws lightly over the arm of his snowsuit. More than that, he looks forward to later, when they're all at home, when the cabin is snug with two fires, the smell of bathwater, and the hum of lanterns. Then, as it thaws behind the stove, he'll take the wolverine, its snarl softening to black, spongy lips, and shape its face into a smile.

Volcano

Julia sat on the living room rug, sewing a button on one of Dave's shirts. It was warm for April–what Dave called a bluebird day–and the sun pouring through the window made her perspire. She un-buttoned the neck of her blouse and rolled up her sleeves. An Alas-kan tan was the *idea* of getting warm through a window, even if the glass blocked out the actual tanning rays.

Fifty-two years old, and she still had good skin. With all the days she'd spent working in the fields and around the yard, she'd never had too much sun.

A dark spot in the corner of the window caught her eye. It was moving, fast–a line of black cloud pushing across the clear sky. It wasn't like any weather she'd ever seen. *Fire!* She tucked her needle into the shirt's cuff and went to the door.

The mushroom shape was just like all the drawings she'd ever seen of nuclear bomb explosions. It rose straight up in a column and then billowed out into a horizontal cap. The sight was so foreign, un-natural, and yet–it was strangely familiar, as though a lifetime of living with the possibility had prepared her. She shut the door and snapped on the radio. Although she couldn't put a name on what she felt, she knew it wasn't fear.

On the radio, the man was saying it over and over again. Volcano, volcano, volcano. The mountain, which had been puffing wisps of steam for months, had blown its top. They didn't know anything more. They were checking with authorities. Stay tuned. The ash was heading this way. It was a good idea to stay inside.

Julia watched the dark cloud sweep east until it passed over the sun, blocking it entirely. Not even a pale circle shone through. The cloud fell like a curtain, cutting off the distance; she could barely make out the grove of cottonwoods at the bottom of the hill. And then the ash began to fall, dirtying the last patches of snow, blotting out all color.

The man repeated the news. They were trying to get more information from the authorities. The best advice they had was to stay put indoors. Don't drive your car. The air filter will clog up.

Julia rolled down her sleeves and resumed her button-sewing. She wasn't going anywhere. She never did go far from the homestead. How could she, when the animals needed to be fed, the cow milked, the chores done? At most, she drove to town three times a week to deliver milk and eggs.

She glanced at the calendar beside the refrigerator. It was marked into blocks—two weeks on and two weeks off. That had been the pattern of Dave's life for years now. Two weeks at Prudhoe Bay, two weeks at home on the homestead. He had only been gone for three days.

She pictured Dave at work, wearing his hardhat, tending some oil-drilling machinery, all of his mind on what he was doing. If he looked up, he'd see the frozen Arctic stretching away to the horizon. He wouldn't know that back home, his fields and home were being buried under volcanic ash.

So there.

Julia snipped her thread. In the dark she could hardly see it, but she didn't want to turn on a light. She sat on the couch and watched the ash fall, like a fine, crystalline snow, past the windows. Pompeii, wasn't it, that was buried in ash, everything neatly preserved, with people curled up sleeping, or sitting at their tables with bowls of food? Ash, or the blast of hot air that shot across the land, crisping everything in its path?

The man on the radio still didn't have much information. The ash was clogging the equipment at the power plant. It was getting into the turbines and damaging them. They were going to have to be shut down. The station would be off the air. There would be no electricity.

And then it was gone. The radio was silent, the refrigerator ground to a stop. She turned off the radio. Her good citizenship—turning off what she could, to save the power system from a surge whenever the electricity came back on—was automatic.

Julia lay on the bed beneath the skylight and watched the ash fall. It settled onto the glass in a coating of small, dark grains. Then a stream avalanched off the roof above and slid down the glass, clearing a path.

She thought, *I can't do anything about a volcano.*

The sky through the cleared track was the deep gray of old tar paper. A night sky, starless, here in the middle of the day, at—she glanced at the clock beside the bed—11:18, but it had said that for more than an hour. She kept forgetting.

She pulled a blanket over her. She missed the familiar sounds she never heard until they stopped. The click of the digital clock as it flipped from one minute to the next. The rattle of the refrigerator. The hum of the lights. The static and occasional chatter of the CB radio that she left on for company more than for messages. Her house had never been so quiet.

She listened to her breathing. She imagined that the volcano kept blowing, belching, spreading its insides across the country. What could you do about a volcano? You couldn't escape it. You couldn't put it out, or clear the ash away as though it were snow.

Over on the bureau, Julia could just make out the children's graduation pictures. She knew them by heart; she didn't need light to see them. David's was cropped around his shoulders so that he looked handsome and whole. You couldn't see the arm that was gone, mangled in a mower when he'd been trying—so hard—to be the man on the homestead, doing more than a boy should have had to do. He did all right with his hook, down in San Diego, considering. Sharon's picture gave her more pain. Even in her smile, you could see the discontent. Sharon couldn't wait to leave the homestead. Oregon,

California, Texas. Julia wasn't sure where her daughter was any-more. She only knew for certain that she wasn't anywhere near cows, muddy roads, or volcanoes.

Without electricity, Dave couldn't reach her. He could phone their friends who lived down on the road, but they couldn't call through by CB radio. Not without electricity.

Julia swung her legs down and walked across the room to the win-dow. Everything she saw, across the fields to the forests and the inlet below, was gray, like a grainy newspaper photograph shot in poor light. Hummocks of dead grass rose and fell into valleys of old snow, the whole hillside as neutral as if it were all one material, like a child's papier-mâché model. The forests were several shades darker, but gray, too—not green—and blurry, as though wrapped in heavy fog. The inlet was lost within the same clouds that obscured the sky—clouds that streaked to the sea the way rainstorms sometimes do. It was colorless—this still photo—absent even of the headlights of cars winding up the coast road, the spots of boats on the water. Everyone was shut down, saving their engines, waiting.

She thought about the chickens in their shed, the cow in the barn. Both doors were open to the yard. If she'd been smart, she'd have shut them earlier. That, and she'd have drawn water and filled every container in the house, instead of sewing that foolish button.

Dave will never wear that shirt again. Julia tried out the thought. It was reasonable. When they came for bodies, when it was all over, they wouldn't bother with household possessions and personal ef-fects. The crew of men with masks over their faces would dig down throught the ash, searching for a door or window. They'd find her in bed, under the darkened skylight.

Already, she had trouble picturing Dave. She tried to focus on the face beneath the hardhat. Smiling, his cheeks bunched up, but then he let his face go, and creases sagged from beneath his eyes and at the edge of his mouth.

Julia rummaged through a drawer and came up with a blue ban-dana. She tied it around her neck. Downstairs, she put on her jacket, pulled the bandana up to cover her mouth and nose, and squeezed through the door.

The air smelled like rotten eggs.

Julia crossed the yard. She tried to pick her feet straight up instead of scuffing; still, they raised clouds of dust. Her eyes stung. She narrowed them until she was looking through the flutter of lashes. In her mouth, ash ground between her molars like leftover polish after a dental cleaning.

The cow was lying down in her stall. She shifted her weight from one hip to another but didn't get up. Julia talked to her for a minute. She told her she would shoot her before she let her suffocate or starve. She owed her that. She pulled the barn door shut and flattened herself against it, thinking, *He's never here when things happen.*

The spring before, someone had set the next hill on fire. The yellow flames, like something alive, had raced through the dead grass toward their homestead. She'd joined the neighbors, beating at the fire with shovels, until her hands were blistered and raw. The flames nearly made it to the fenceline. When Dave's two weeks were over, her hands were healed, and new grass had grown up to cover the burn.

In the fall, alder banks slid down and blocked their road. Wind blew the chimney off. Later, snowstorms struck; she shoveled, plowed, chained up the truck to get through. By the time Dave came back, everything was cleared and repaired. It was no good wanting to tell him, *It was too much work for me. You should have been here.* The weather would already have turned to rain, snow melted into nothing.

In the chicken house, the chickens were quiet. Julia crouched in their doorway and saw them all roosted together in the far corner, their feathers fluffed out. They thought it was night.

The kitchen clock gave the same stopped time. Julia knew it would never run again. What was time, anyway? Twenty-seven years on the homestead. All those years of coping, taking charge of what needed to be done. Was this what she'd been waiting for?

She found a damp washcloth in the bathroom and wiped the grime from her face. Her eyes still hurt, and she made herself cry to wash them out. She liked what she saw in the mirror. This was how she should look in the end—quiet tears, no hysteria, stoicism mixed with regret. She raised a hand to arrange a lock of hair more tragically. It was thick and stiff, coated with volcano dirt.

She tied the bandana over her head. The look was right.

In the kitchen, Julia pulled out a chair and sat at the table. The things she'd meant to do – baking bread, vacuuming, walking the west fence to see where the moose had knocked it down – were no longer possible. She supposed she could always light a candle to see by; she could continue her mending. That was what she always did – continue, go on, as though nothing ever changed.

She didn't move to light a candle. She sat and thought. *It has come to wanting a disaster that is beyond anything I can handle. A volcano is bigger than both of us.*

Through the front window, the clouds changed to a lighter shade of gray. A dark edge broke abruptly to a sliver of blue. The cottonwoods sharpened within their ghostly outlines. Julia turned away from the window.

The refrigerator rumbled as its motor started up; the house began to hum. Julia ignored the sounds. Her eyes were on the wall calendar. She studied it and smoldered.

Nature Lessons

Mary was watching the view through the train window, her hands clasped against stiff new jeans. Marco wondered what details she was drawn to; as far as he could tell, she was staring at the forests hurrying by. He studied the round, blond top of her head, the way her hair was pulled back from her face in tight braids that were then woven into a pair of larger ones. The elaborate braiding was Anna's work, of course. Already, from being slept on, it was unraveling; strands hung loose at both her forehead and the nape of her neck, making her look a little less doll-like, a little more like a real ten-year-old.

Mary shifted in her seat, turning to face him. "It was so light last night. Doesn't it ever get dark around here?"

Marco smiled. "Not in the summer. We're so far north, and the earth's axis is tilted like this." He made an earth with one fist and indicated the sun with his other, open hand. "Pretend my fingers are curled around the axis, and here's Alaska up here. The earth rotates like this." She wasn't watching. Her eyes had swept across his demonstration and on out the window. "In the winter it's the opposite. It's dark most of the time," he ended feebly.

"We had it in our science book," she said, "the way everything goes around the sun." She brought her gaze back through the window, to the child coloring across the aisle. "Mercury, Mars, Saturn, Pluto, Neptune . . ." She scrunched her face.

Marco had known them in order once. There was a saying, like "All good boys deserve fudge" for the lines in music and Roy G. Biv for the colors of the spectrum. "Venus," he said.

"Don't tell me!" She reached to put a hand over his mouth. "I'm thinking. I'll get them."

"Okay," he said, sitting back. He couldn't think of the others anyway. He knew there were more, but he couldn't remember how many. Later, he'd ask her the seven dwarfs. He knew that. Most people forgot Doc, at least.

While he waited for her to finish thinking, he watched the passing landscape. He'd traveled it so often, back and forth to town for supplies or a stint of work, and yet he never could get over its changing beauty. It was so wild—all mountains and gorges, forests and brush, rivers foaming, waterfalls cascading to pools. As they moved from sunlight to shade to sunlight again under the sheeplike clouds, he admired its richness—the greens overtaking the subtleties of spring, the purple lupine intertwining. The colors had brightened, just in the two days he'd been gone.

Yesterday, waiting at the airport, he'd spent quite a while looking at the display of ducks that, along with other stuffed wildlife, was one of the tourist attractions. You could always find some Japanese people lined up in front of the bear, taking pictures of each other. He thought how sad it was that that was as close as most people ever got to nature. He couldn't stand for his daughter to grow up thinking animals were what you saw mounted in plastic boxes or in zoos, not when she could watch moose browsing or sandhill cranes circling overhead.

That's what made it so hard to be apart from her for so long, and why he'd fought as hard as he had for custody rights, never giving up. Ironically, it was also why he had had such a hard time getting the court to let him have her at all. Anna and her lawyers kept trying to paint him as some kind of weirdo who lived out in the woods in a shack, a caveman or something. When he proved that he actually had a well-built cabin with a stove that kept it warm, that he cooked food and read books like a normal human being, and that an outhouse could be quite civilized, with a door and a window and toilet paper on a roll, they still said it was too far from any medical facilities and otherwise "inappropriate."

But he'd won, gradually—first the right to take her places "Outside," and now the right to bring her home for a few weeks. After this he'd win the right for *her* to decide where she wanted to live, how to divide her year between her mother and her father, Los Angeles and the Alaskan bush.

Mary nudged him in the side. "Do you know how to play Hangman?" she asked.

Marco remembered the stick figure, body parts added as wrong letters were guessed. It wasn't one of his favorite games, even as a kid. "You may have to help me with the rules," he said. "It's been a long time."

"That's okay." Mary dug through her canvas bag. Pulling out a pencil and a pad of lined paper, she showed him a name and number on the top sheet. "Do you know these people?"

Marco looked at it. The number had an Anchorage prefix. "No. Who is it?"

Mary shrugged. "I don't know. Mom gave it to me. It's some friend of someone she knows."

"How come she gave it to you? Are you supposed to call them or something?"

"No. It was just in case you weren't at the airport."

Marco struck his fist against his thigh. No wonder Mary had looked so anxious and teary-eyed when she arrived; Anna had told her that her father, that weirdo-hippie, would probably forget to show up. "C'mon," he said, making himself smile, "you didn't really think I wouldn't be there, did you?"

Mary was carefully drawing a noose and the spaces for letters, and she didn't answer. Her tongue just showed between her lips as she concentrated.

The train rounded a curve, and Marco could see in the distance the unnamed mountain around which he had framed one of his windows. "Look!" he said. "That mountain up there, that's where we're going." But already the train had finished its curve and pushed the mountain back out of sight.

"Go ahead," Mary said. "Pick a letter."

The train's clatter was gradually absorbed by the wilderness, until the only sounds were their own rustlings and the chirps and flutters of a flock of sparrows in the alders beside the track. Marco lashed Mary's suitcase to his packframe, cursing Anna beneath his breath. He'd *told* her that Mary should bring everything she needed in a backpack; instead, she'd sent her with an enormous suitcase plus the canvas bag. He'd fashioned some straps for the bag last night so that Mary could wear that, at least. The rest of his load – the supplies he'd bought in town – would have to wait for a second trip.

As he hoisted the packframe to his shoulders, he saw Mary slap at her wrist. "Mosquito?"

Mary scratched at the spot. "I guess so."

"Let's see," he said, pulling up her shirt collar to cover her neck. "I didn't think to bring any repellant. If we just keep moving, they won't be able to keep up with us. They're pretty sluggish beasts, really."

Marco led the way, stepping over roots and around tight, bushy corners, trying to go slowly and keep an eye on Mary's progress. It was hard for him to shorten his stride. After a few minutes he waited for Mary to catch up. "This was a game trail originally – that's why it's so curvy," he said. "If we were birds, it would be a lot shorter." Mary trudged toward him, her arms swinging like a pair of pistons. "You're a good hiker."

"We did this in Brownies," she said. "Only we sang songs."

"So sing me a song," he said.

She sang "The Ants Go Marching One by One." Marco joined in, self-consciously. *Hoorah! Hoorah!* Usually he moved quickly but quietly along the trail, listening for the drop of leaves or the hoots of a grouse. *The little one stops to suck its thumb.* He remembered the words from his own camp days, surprised they were still the same.

"Now you pick one," she said.

He thought. Remembering songs wasn't a strong point with him. He thought of the Beatles. "Rocky Raccoon" – yeah! He sang the whole thing, humming a bit where he couldn't remember words. When he was done he turned to look at Mary. "How'd you like that one?"

"I never heard it before."

"What? Never?" Marco was incredulous. "You don't know who sang that?" Mary didn't answer. He could hear her breathing behind him as she worked to keep up. "That's the Beatles. You know the Beatles, don't you?"

"Yeah, they were like the Monkees. I've seen them on TV."

"You saw the Beatles on TV?"

"No, the Monkees, silly. I think the Beatles died."

For a moment Marco wondered if they had, if some conspiracy had blown them all away one week when he was upriver or somewhere away from the radio. He would have heard, though, something that important. "No," he said. "They quit making records together, and John was killed. Only John Lennon was killed, shot by a crazy person."

They walked in silence for a while. "It was incredible," Marco said. "It was a cultural revolution, really. Their music turned the world on its head. Every boy in America wanted a Beatles haircut—we got thrown out of school for it. It was wild."

"You got thrown out of school?" Mary sounded doubtful.

"For having hair too long." Marco laughed. "Too long meant it went past my ears." He turned to grin at Mary, tugging on the end of his ponytail where it hung over his shoulder. She still looked concerned. "I was in the seventh grade. I only missed two days. All across America we were growing our hair and listening to the Beatles."

Marco stopped short, pointing to a tree trunk lying next to the trail. "Look," he said. "Here's your first nature lesson. That's fox scat. You can tell 'cause foxes like to do it up high. You always find their shits on top of things."

Mary stood back on the trail. "Looks like dogdoo to me."

"But, look." Marco picked up a twig and poked at the scat, breaking it apart. "See how it's full of hair. That's because it's been eating mice."

"Yuck," Mary said. "How can you touch that? C'mon, I'm getting bit."

Marco hurried on, outdistancing the mosquitoes again. There would be plenty of time for nature lessons later. He resisted pointing out the just-forming watermelon berries and the yellow spears of skunk cabbage. Later, they'd make a collection, pressing specimens into a book. It would be fun, like being a kid again, to share that with her.

"Well, we're home," Marco said. He surveyed the cabin in the clearing, imagining that he was seeing it for the first time. It looked so domestic, its log walls rising protectively, the sod roof weighted with grasses. The woodpile was comfortably large, the splitting block surrounded by wood chips like flecks of sunlight. With the garden, behind, and the outbuildings, it looked like a sort of oasis in the wilderness, a pastoral mingling of Man and Nature. Mary had seen pictures, of course, but it needed the rest–the twitters of birds, the smell of sunlight warming the earth, the clean air–to be complete. "Is it what you expected?" he asked.

"I guess so," she said. She was already at the door, figuring out the latch system.

Inside, he heated water on the propane burner to make soup. He sliced some bread, first removing the spots of mold that had developed while he was away. "This is sourdough bread," he said. "Do you know what sourdough is?"

Mary nodded and blew on her soup. "We have it at home. We eat it all the time. Sourdough French bread, with spaghetti."

"I bet you never made your own, from sourdough starter."

Mary shook her head.

"We'll do that, tomorrow or the next day."

"Yeah, I guess you can't just go to the store and buy what you want like regular people." She laughed.

"No," Marco said. Regular. He heard it as though Anna had said it, meaning normal: *But, Judge, it's not normal to live out in the middle of the Alaskan wilderness.* "No, we're not very regular here. This is another kind of life, where we do things for ourselves."

Mary, stirring her soup, watched her spoon. Marco knew he sounded self-righteous. But he also knew he was right, that this was what it all came down to–a choice of lives. And he knew he could convince her, with time. Half the genes were his, after all; the potential was there. Anna just had a head start. He had the next two weeks. He ate the last of his bread. "I'll be an hour or so getting the other load. I take it you've had enough hike for one day?"

Mary nodded, then stifled a yawn.

"Well, make yourself at home then. You'll be sleeping up in the loft, if you want to put your things away there. The outhouse is around to the left." He pointed through one of the windows. "If you go out, you better stay in the clearing, until you get to know the area better."

"Don't worry," she said. "I'm not going out *there*."

When Marco returned, breaking from the trees into sunlight, the cabin looked absolutely cheerful. Knowing that Mary was there, waiting for him, was like coming back on a cold winter day and seeing smoke from his banked fire curling from the chimney. Only this was better.

It was perfectly quiet when he entered. Mary was sprawled face-down across the foam pads that he called a couch, sneakered feet toward the door, head hung over the far end so that her body seemed to end with the round of her thin shoulders. Marco chuckled to himself. Kids were so damned adaptable. They could sleep anywhere. He tiptoed over to look at her.

"Jeez!" She jerked, rolling to face him and pulling the headphones down around her neck. "What are you doing? You scared me."

Marco backed away. The tinny music spilled into the air. "I thought you were asleep."

Mary sat up all the way. "I got these for my birthday. Want to listen? It's Michael Jackson." She started to take the headphones off.

"No thanks," Marco said, and then, not to seem ungrateful, "not right now. I've got to unpack some stuff."

"I already unpacked mine." Mary put the headphones back on and lay down again.

That evening, after Mary had gone to bed, Marco inspected the garden and dug listlessly at a few weeds. Probably he'd simply expected too much. He should have remembered that she was the same child who, last year when they went to Baja, hadn't wanted to get sand in her shoes and who was most enamored by a plastic hairbrush that had washed up on the beach. *He* had been the one to collect the bleached pelican skulls, the long bills as delicate as fine china, that now embellished a cabin wall. "Oh, those," she'd said, when he'd pointed them out earlier. "You save the wierdest things."

A year older, her tastes had solidified that much more into mainstream America. Too, she was that much closer to becoming a teenager, with all the cliquishness and gimmickry that involved. Tonight, tucking her in beneath a sleeping bag, he'd felt awkward with his hug. He'd missed so many of the hugging years; it was hard to resume now, when she was almost past being the child that need-ed it. A couple more years, when she'd sprouted breasts and attract-ed gangly, pimpled boyfriends, it would be even harder. What role would be left for him then?

Marco lit a joint. Dinner had been okay. He'd cooked a bearmeat stew. She hadn't really liked the meat but she'd chewed at it bravely, pushing aside only the bigger chunks. After, they played cribbage. Then he thought they might just sit and talk, but she was fidgety, wanting to be entertained. She had a book of trivia and asked him questions. They were dumb, questions about movie stars he'd nev-er heard of or athletes who threw so many touchdown passes.

He ground out the joint on the fencepost and dropped it into his pocket. She hadn't noticed the marijuana plants in the greenhouse. Or she hadn't said anything. Surely she would recognize them? He didn't know what she thought of pot, but he knew that Anna would disapprove. He'd keep his smoking low-profile.

An owl hooted, and Marco walked back behind the garden and down toward the spring to look for it. It was a great horned, sitting at the top of a dead spruce. Silhouetted against the night sky, its ear tufts fanned as it turned one way and then the other. Watching it filled him with a sense of reverence. It was these moments, these encounters with God's other creatures, that he valued most about living in the woods. It was this he wanted Mary to know, this that was important, this that had value. He turned quietly and started back, thinking of how he would lift her, bundled in covers, and carry her gently to the tree. Half-asleep, misted with dreams, she'd listen with him, setting her own internal rhythm to that of the patient bird. Smoothing her brow with his hand, he'd draw her eyes open.

Passing the garden, he slowed his step. He'd scared her once to-day, tiptoeing through the cabin. He couldn't risk it again. These things took time. He sat down against the woodpile; the owl kept calling, again and again, at the same intervals. It was only the first day. He watched the sky deepen until, at last, silence met the dark.

Marco held the can of tomato sauce while Mary finished spreading the dough in the pan. It was hard for her, to push and stretch the dough without tearing it, and Marco could see that she was getting frustrated. She would do it, though. He liked her persistence.

"Mary Alicia," he said.

"What?"

"Nothing. I just like saying your name." He had taken to calling her by both her names, and she hadn't objected, although he knew she never used her middle name back in L.A. He'd never liked the name Mary; it had been Anna's choice. "Have you ever thought of spelling your name differently?"

Seriously intent on the pizza, she gave him a quick look to see if he was kidding. "Like what?"

"I once knew a woman whose name was Merry. M-e-r-r-y. She was a very joyful person. When she came into a room, it was almost like hearing bells ring, Christmas bells."

"I know a girl named Noelle." Mary pushed the finished pan across the table to him, and he handed her some mushrooms to slice. She was looking more relaxed, at least, taking on some of the tempo and character of the bush, fitting to its walking speed and raggedness. With her hair in ordinary pigtails and a dusting of flour on her shirtfront, she looked right at home. Marco was amused, too, by the faint orange glow at each corner of her mouth, left by a glass of Tang. It made her look like she was smiling.

The mushrooms were a benefit of all the rain, unseasonable for June. Bad weather had kept them indoors more than Marco had expected, had prevented them from doing all the things he'd planned. Still, one day they hiked to a trout stream and caught some fish. Other days they collected edible plants. Mary turned out to be an aggressive weeder, and the garden had never looked so good.

It nagged at Marco, the sense that Mary was indulging him in his activities rather than enjoying them herself. She never complained or resisted, but she never embraced anything they did with any degree of enthusiasm. It seemed a passive sort of cooperation, like the dutiful scout march of the first day. When they were done cutting wood or picking nettles, he felt an unspoken sigh of relief. She didn't protest the rain, content enough to curl up inside with her tapes or the radio or some puzzle books she'd brought along. Marco thought of prisoners or hospital patients, people who did the best they could while waiting for their day of release.

Mary laid the mushroom pieces down evenly over the cheese. She sighed. "It's not exactly Pizza Hut's."

"You bet it's not," Marco said. "Moosemeat's too much of a delicacy for Pizza Hut."

Mary picked up a piece of mushroom from the table as though she were going to eat it, then put it back down. "I like pepperoni the best." Then she told him, again, the whole long list of foods she would eat as soon as she got home. ". . . And a big glass of Pepsi, with lots of ice cubes. And a hot fudge sundae." She smacked her lips.

Marco sat stiffly, watching the country roll by. It was far too short, two weeks. He never saw another owl, one to share with her. And they never saw a moose. He couldn't seem to hold her attention with the small flowers or the places on the trees where porcupines had eaten the bark.

Mary tossed in her seat, swinging her pigtails, trying to see everything in the train at once. "Look at that woman," she whispered noisily to Marco. "I like her glasses. If I had to get glasses, I'd get them like that." The favored glasses had curved earpieces and a sort of plaque announcing the designer's name. Mary turned around to follow a conversation behind them, half-standing to see; her hands jerked in her lap.

Marco couldn't help smiling. She was like a speed freak, all movement and mouth. He'd seen the same transformation in other people—even in himself, to a degree. After the stillness of the bush, being with a crowd in a changing landscape was a sort of sensory overload. The colors all looked brighter; the chaos and variety overwhelmed.

"I can hardly wait," she said. "You'll buy me a double-scooper, won't you?"

"Whatever you want."

"I want one butter pecan, and one mint chocolate chip. Or maybe walnut fudge. I don't know. I can't decide. What are you going to have?"

Marco rubbed his chin. "Chocolate?"

"Two scoops of the same?"

"Probably. I like chocolate."

"Are you a chocoholic?"

"I doubt it."

Mary pulled her pad of paper from her bag and began writing down ice cream flavors. Then she flipped the page back and drew a picture of a big fish standing on its tail. "You haven't been to Sea World, have you?" she asked. She had already mentioned, several times, that she was going there in August, with her mother.

Marco wanted to say "Screw Sea World. Stay with me and I'll show you some real orcas, not ones that balance balls on their noses." He didn't, though. He was learning that, impossible as it seemed, there were people who preferred to see the ones in tanks. Instead he asked, "What will you tell people about your trip up here?"

Mary made an exaggerated show of thinking, much as she had that first day when they talked about the earth's tilt and the planets. "I'll talk about hiking on the trail"—she bobbed her head, dipping one shoulder and then the other in an imitation of a fast walk—"to get there and all the different things we ate. I'll talk about how you shot a bear and once floated down a river all alone for a month without seeing anyone."

Marco was struck by the choices of the bear encounter and the river trip, both of which happened well before her arrival and that she'd only heard about.

"People will think I shot the bear while you were here. Is that what you want them to think?"

She laughed. "No way. I'll say we ate the meat that you put in jars, from when you killed the bear before."

"Even though you didn't like it?"

"I won't say I *liked* it."

"What other things will you say that you did?"

"Oh, I don't know." Mary slid back on the seat. "I'll say I was with my *dad*." She put both of her hands around Marco's arm and squeezed tightly, snuggling against his side.

Marco reached to cover her small hands with his free one. Before he could, she let him go and turned, bouncing, to look at something in the back of the car. Marco stared at the rough hand that he held open before him and then, because he could think of nothing else, laid it down on his arm where hers had been.

Small Potatoes

I make my own trail, not because it's quicker but because there's more to see. I don't do it enough anymore, traipsing through with an eye for rose hips or for the spider's snare with its lump of fluttering, tormented moth. As I bend branches, I'm comforted that there is still so much unfenced and untrammeled space. It hasn't come to that yet, that people here feel the need to mark it off and use it up.

Even as a little girl in Boston, I was looking for this. The day I learned about the Westward Movement—settlers trundling along in covered wagons, as it was presented—I raced around after school, drunk with the concept of first steps into unknown territory, stamping my feet into any unblemished patch of snow, shouting "Pioneer! Pioneer! Pioneer!"

When I came to Alaska, it was with the sure knowledge that here were places that, truly, no one had stepped. And it mattered, the sense of putting a foot down and knowing I was the first to look upon the world from exactly that vantage point. Every sight—of mountain or mouse hole—was a discovery.

You said it was the same for you, growing up in the Midwest. When we met, it was as though we'd once been members of the same backyard club, sisters who shared a coded language. When you spoke, it was as though you were saying my own thoughts. I felt we were resuming a friendship instead of beginning one.

That first summer, working together in the cannery, I lived in my tent and you lived in your van. Days off, we mucked about in the bay after clams, caking ourselves with mud that dried to a ghost-gray skin. Other times we hiked into the hills to fields of chamomile we picked for tea. I wonder if you still think about the day we walked the bluff's edge, weaving back around the ravines and then on out to the points of land where fireweed rippled in the sea breeze. Eagles rode the thermals above us, and we watched two at play, diving at each other and once locking talons as they tumbled above us. We agreed we both wanted to be birds in our next lives.

Now that the cold has come, causing the country to lie down and curl up around itself, it's easier to get through here. Only a couple of weeks ago, the trees and bushes were still lunging around, frothing with fevered leaves and seed, stretching, the grasses dizzy over my head. Now the exuberance is gone, leaving jaundiced alders, berries fallen or pinched to skin, grasses pale and brittle as though the frost has sucked the green resilience out of them. Yesterday's wind has turned the remaining leaves to bare their undersides like submissive bellies; it's flattened the grasses so they all lie in one direction. I bully my way through, kicking loose the snarls that catch my feet. The morning's frost flakes off and sprinkles down.

It's only when I reach the highway that the sun clears the trees. It's warmer, instantly, and I pause to unzip my jacket at the throat. It's early and a Saturday; there's no traffic this far out the road. Most people are still waking up, drinking coffee beside stoked stoves and staring out windows at reminders of chores to be done before freeze-up: gardens to be turned, skirting to be nailed, wood to be split and stacked. The first hard frost, no matter how late, always comes before any of us is ready. In homes up and down the road, lists—the must-dos of fall—are being assembled.

You, too, will have your list, that you've brought from Anchorage: weatherstripping to stick to the bottom of the door, mouse-traps to set, a load of firewood to arrange for delivery. Your list is different from the rest of ours, now that you come only on an occasional weekend. It's not the list of buttoning-up, of drawing shelter close like a wrap of sweater. Instead, it's a list of absentee fixes, of purchases. The mousetraps will bang shut in the silence after you, catless, have closed the door behind you; the wood will arrive one day, heaved from the back of a pickup to lie in a pile at your doorstep like a yardful of stumps.

Walking along the empty road, I think again of the eagles that tumbled with locked talons, the day we discovered the old log cabin. It stood just at the edge of the bluff, ramshackle, the roof partly fallen in and the windows broken out. I poked my head through an opening and smelled the damp rot that was somehow satisfying in its earthiness. "Move," you said in your eager way and slung a leg over the splintered sill. We pawed through the debris, and you dug out an old spoon, tarnished green. Later, we sat outside, chewing on chives we found clumped against a wall, trailing them from our mouths like strings of licorice. We wondered who had lived there and where they had gone, and what it must have been like to have settled this land before the roads came through. Just as we wanted to be birds the next time around, we decided we'd been Indians, or explorers, or calicoed prairie wives before; we felt that much affinity for the open country.

This trip, besides your list of to-dos, you'll bring other things—groceries, cleaning supplies, new candles. You'll also have a second list—items you've decided you need in Anchorage and want to remember to take back. I've watched this ebb and flow between your two households. In comes the sack of groceries, out goes the smaller bag of garbage you'll drop in the dumpster as you pass through town. In comes the new broom. Out go the favorite chamois shirt, the binoculars, the game of Scrabble, the bread knife, and the vegetarian cookbook.

When you made the decision to work in Anchorage, that's just how you put it—you would work there, but it was temporary, a job away from home. Home would remain here, and you'd get back to it on weekends, as often as you could. You'd only be "camping out" in your furnished apartment, drinking out of jelly jars and browning toast in the oven. Your real, complete, household would be here, waiting.

I've watched it happen, though, the ebb of possessions. It's not like tides anymore, a wash in and out; it's like the flood of a river now. Every trip you take away more, emptying the house of those things that make it most yours. Load by load, you're moving away.

When I turn off to your place, I study the ruts, wondering if you're really here. You said you would be, when we talked. "This weekend for sure," you said, sounding guilty, regretful. "I want to spend some time with you. We'll pick cranberries. Plan on it."

It's funny in a way, how we've stayed so close through everything. Always, our friendship endured. We both looked for men to share our lives with, and expected that someday we would. I suppose I was jealous when you began spending so much time with Ron. And for me there was Patrick, and Mike, and Galen. They were all good men—yours and mine—but then you and I would always find ourselves together again, across one of our kitchen tables, drinking tea and talking. Every time it was as though we were finally able to communicate in the same language again, after having tried to get by with foreigners. I remember telling you about Galen and football and fishing. I had told him, while he was watching football on television, that I was going to hike down to the river to fish. He told me to wait—he would drive me down when the game was over. I didn't need to tell you that what I really wanted was the walk, that fishing was an excuse to carry a rod down and back through the woods, that I had to feel guilty because he offered a ride I didn't want, and then that he accused me of trying to rush him away from his game. You were already nodding; you knew exactly what I'd meant to begin with and what he would say, and even that the last three minutes of the game would go on and on.

The men came and went, for each of us, but neither of us ever found one that was a friend in the way we were to each other, someone with whom we could talk, saying everything without insult or doubt or misunderstanding and knowing what the other meant.

And now, each of us is by herself.

The ruts don't tell me much. The mud's frozen hard, tire tracks printed in it. Where it was wettest, it's crystallized like quartz, pointed spears of brown ice radiating from each pit. They crunch under my feet, shattering. It's clear that no one has driven in or out this morning.

The low light has that luminescent quality, as though it were slipping under the sides of things, filling them from within. The bent grasses along the road glow yellow; frost melting to dew magnifies in beads along the edges. You always used to remark on it, summer evenings when the light slanted in from the north, washing the trees and fields with an underwater greenness.

When I reach the top of the rise, I can see the roof of your house. The shakes catch the sunlight the same as the grass, the cedar burnished like gold. But it's the chimney I watch. Straining my sight against the wall of spruce that rises behind, I look for the wavy distortion the heat from a dampered, smokeless fire causes. The trees stand still as a painted backdrop, and I know that you're not here after all.

You're busy, I know. Things come up. It's hard to get away. You would be here if you could, pulling muffins from the oven and pouring springwater into your kettle.

I keep walking toward your house. As it materializes, top to bottom, I think how systematically it went the other way, the summer you built it. I'm still amazed at the assurance with which you did it. When you started you didn't even know the names of what you needed—joists or studs, rafters or siding. They were all just boards to you. The times I came to help, it was "Cut all those boards to look like this" and "Use those big nails over there." You knew exactly what you wanted, as if by instinct. And when it was done, one board nailed to the next, it was one solid piece—no holes, nothing extra sticking out.

Seven years later, there it is—still standing, still surprising me. With time, the rough-cut spruce, once so banana blond, has grayed to distinction. It reminds me of a Wyeth painting, with its patina of fog and seclusion.

In the beginning, when we moved to the hill, the places we found were simple and rough. Yours was a homestead cabin, with an uneven floor that sloped downhill. A pencil dropped in the kitchen rolled to the door, and in wet weather water seeped up through the floorboards. My place was less historically pleasing—plywood, its walls lined with cardboard from cases of beer. I tightened it up with some ceiling insulation, installed a barrel stove, and spent winter nights reading by a kerosene lamp. Later, when you built your own place, I settled into my rental in the trees. We joked about my electricity and your sheetrock. "It's real uptown," we said. "We better watch out that we don't get citified."

Your top story stares at me first, the two south windows like eyes flashing, the smaller one caught in a wink. Beneath it more windows, none matching, line either side of the L. The short leg thrusts forward, throwing a small shadow like a wedge of night against the longer. You did right with the angles, capturing the best of the winter sun and avoiding the flat, spiritless faces common to new construction. The porch, along the side, adds an air of leisure and comfort, as though it might be hung with an old-fashioned wicker swing.

As I get closer, the look of desertion looms larger. The road cuts away, with the spur into your yard crowded from both sides by grass. The center strip of weeds stands firm; months have passed since it's been pushed over by the belly of a car. The yard, too, grows wild: nettles collapsed over the splitting block, a dry pushki stalk parting the legs of a sawhorse.

I climb the steps, the sound of my boots a thudding of arrival. The door is padlocked. I tug on the lock, testing. When it holds, I move down the porch, nudging with my foot at a coffee can along the way. It's empty except for a stiff paintbrush.

Framing my gloved hands around my eyes, I press against the window to see inside. Plates and cups are stacked on a dish towel beside the sink, ready to be put away. There's a fancy cookie tin and a stick of margarine on the counter. Beyond the wood stove I can see the edge of a chair and some magazines—*New Yorkers*—scattered on the floor; their covers are like fall leaves—one mostly orange, another green and yellow. Ragg socks lie where they were pulled heel over toe.

My breath—I've tried to hold it in—finally steams up my space in the window. The interior pulls away as though masked by a cloud.

It's part of your plan, I know, to leave it every time like this—odds and ends of food and clothing lying around—so that when you return it feels like coming home, as though you've never really left.

"I can't eat the scenery." It's what you said when you took the job in Anchorage. You were joking, sort of—parodying what the business people said when they argued for more, faster growth. We both knew what the choice was—money and some professional achievement instead of the space and self-sufficiency and, yes, scenery that was ours here. Now you dress in suits and nylons and sit at a desk, reviewing plans and writing up reports. You told me that you don't even have a window in your office, and that the traffic after work is hell.

There's sacrifice either way, of course. Living here, I'll never be rich or influential. I'll never be quoted in the newspaper twice in a week; in fact, I may not even manage to read the paper twice in a week. Waking to knead bread and collect eggs from the henhouse, my days fill with mundane essentials. Instead of waiting in a traffic jam, I may spend an entire winter day chaining up my car and winching it through snowdrifts to the road. My words fall into cliché, howdy-do, and the sluggish thought that goes with chatter in the post office line or reporting to the cats at home. Work is what I can find, always strictly for money as I support a lifestyle the way others support too many children.

Sitting on the edge of your porch, I let my legs dangle. I look back the way I came, across to the mountains. Snowfields divide the pale sky from the water below as though bleeding off the color, draining it down the cracked and broken glaciers to the concentrate, undiluted blue of bay. There's never a time watching the mountains that I don't marvel at where I live, and I cannot imagine living where I couldn't watch the snowline rise and fall with the seasons.

And when I look around me again, I see the fenceposts of your garden. There it is, the old plot, looking small and indistinguishable from the rest of the field except for the gray posts that tilt like lightning-struck trees above the grass. Its chicken wire sags from one post to the next; moose, walking through, have pulled it free. In one corner, where it's still strung high, weeds—some climbing vines—have laced it together.

That's all that's left of the garden you turned by hand, layering in truckloads of horse manure and seaweed. You were so proud of what you grew—the early radishes, the chard, the heads of cabbage soft and leathery as medicine balls. I helped you dig potatoes when the plants lay limp over the hills and the soil was cold in our hands; they were small that year, the season short. Perfect for boiling, you said, content with what you had.

When was that, that all that happened—that the fireweed sneaked back across the fenceline as though it had never been spaded under, that the chicken wire loosened and the posts were heaved out by frost? All that's left looks so *old,* I can't believe it has anything to do with us. Somehow, we've become the ones who came before, as much a part of the past as the early homesteaders at the edge of the bluff or the later ones with sunken floors and cardboard walls.

Although you've left and I'm still here, the time when our lives were new and as brilliant as bright nails and fresh-sawn lumber is behind us both. Our first steps through—finding our ways along trails we parted, past rows we planted, up steps we hammered together—are history. I go on, holding to the vision, but I know now that you'll never be so satisfied again with small potatoes.

I drop down off the edge of the porch, landing harder than I expect. I've sat too long, stiffening. I walk over to the garden and around one side. The vine, I think, may be some surviving peas, but it's not; it's nothing I recognize, the leaves scalloped and tinted red, as though they've rusted over. I step across the fence and kick through the grass, searching for some sign. It's all weeds, as far as I can tell, the same as beyond the fence. I step out again and start back toward your house, wondering where I can find something to write a note with—charcoal, wax, anything—but there's nothing here, in this yard grayed out, gone to seed.

Instead, halfway back, I stop and pick some weeds: stalks of fireweed still stuck with wisps of fluff; brittle mare's tail; a handful of grasses fringed with seed cases; the paperlike shell of some cup-shaped flower; a spiky pushki head, each pod spread like a parasol. I place them, inelegant and unarranged, in the paintbrush's can and set the whole bouquet against your door. When you come—whenever you come—they'll be waiting, frozen in time. Although snow may have buried the country, smoothing this morning's rugged beauty into flat, forgetful obliteration, these will stay as now, a reminder to you of what came before.

A True Story

Here is a true story:

In 1971, when I was nineteen years old, seven college friends and I drove from Massachusetts to Alaska. We drove to Fairbanks and then flew, first in a mail plane to a village airstrip, and then in two trips in a float plane, to a lake in the mountains of the Brooks Range. For three weeks we hiked, camped, and scrambled up mountains; then we floated downriver in rubber rafts, through and eventually out of the wilderness.

My memories of that summer are the most idyllic of my life. The sun circled high overhead, barely blinking behind the ring of mountains during what passed for night. Caribou, heels clicking, trotted past our campsites. We belayed ourselves up granite ridges to look down into nameless valleys so beautiful they made me cry.

All these years later, I recall with perfect clarity a whole scrapbook of precise, photographic memories: a carpet of lemon-colored blossoms, the surprised dive of a snow bunting from a rock crevice as I reached for a handhold, a hanging glacier's ceramic blue face.

On the river, we wound back and forth between fireweed-lined banks. The air was soft and grainy, the sun a golden glow; somewhere to the south, forest fires burned. Wolf pups wrestled on a sandbar; as we drifted past, they stopped to stare at us, their over-sized ears stiffening into alertness. Loons flapped and kicked across the water, launching themselves into flight.

I thought I had found the best place on earth.

It was a place that, except for our small group of visitors, was without people.

I went back east, back to school. When I told family and friends about Alaska, I told them about the glaciered mountains and the wolf pups and the fireweed that bloomed along the river. For me, that was the true, the only, story.

I was nineteen. What did I know? I had my head in books or, looking up, my eyes on clouds and mountains. My life was safe and secure, free of any real trouble. I had little idea how other people lived. What I found in Alaska I put into the only context I knew. For the rest, for all I could understand of it, it might never have happened.

There is, in fact, more to the true story. In the end, we left the wilderness.

It was a gradual exit, our float out of the mountains, down a widening river. We began to see signs of other people: abandoned cabins, tree stumps, a sandbar campsite with a scorched log. At length we approached an Athabascan village. The sounds of hammering and barking dogs reached us first. Then, the village itself came into view: wooden skiffs lined the shore like parked cars, blue gas barrels bloomed from weed patches, a sheet fluttered on a line. In the trees at the top of the bluff, we could see a row of log houses. No one seemed to notice us drift by.

At the airstrip just downriver from the village, we unloaded our rafts and pulled them from the water. We pitched our tents and laid out the deflated rafts to dry. The next day, a plane would come and take us away.

Some of us decided to walk back to the village, along a path that crossed a grassy field and entered trees, where it joined a raised boardwalk and continued along the top of the bluff, between the row of houses and the river.

The mood among us was somber. We had come, after all, to the end of our adventure. Each of our thoughts, I'm sure, was turned toward home—family, other friends, waiting jobs, school again in the fall. For me, it had been a perfect trip, but I was only just realizing that it was *only* a trip; wilderness travel was not a way a person could live forever, not a life.

Small, tanned, cherub-faced children ran past us along the boardwalk, dragging sticks that clicked against the breaks between planks. They turned shy when we said hello. An old woman trudged by with an armful of clothes and avoided looking at us. We were acutely aware that we were strangers, uninvited and, for all we knew, resented.

The village seemed unusually still for the time of day. The late-afternoon sun was high in the sky, but the smoke-haze in the air made it seem later, or darker. Aside from the woman and a glimpse of someone sweeping dust through a quickly closed doorway, we didn't see any other adults.

Teenagers, though, were gathered on the boardwalk, smoking cigarettes, jostling one another. We passed a pack of young women wearing blue eyeshadow, combs jutting from the back pockets of tight bell-bottom jeans. We said hello. They answered us, friendly enough, and their long, straight, raven hair swung away from their faces, revealing dangling earrings. A young man in a fringed leather jacket walked past with a portable tape deck turned up loud: Jimi Hendrix. Another group, with another tape deck, followed behind him, and Neil Young overtook Hendrix. A girl with pink fingernails threw down a cigarette and ground it out under a striped running shoe. We exchanged more greetings.

One of them finally pulled us aside, wanting to talk. He was, maybe, sixteen, with a few dark hairs over his lip. A braided leather headband circled his head, exposing the tops of puckish ears. "Hey, man," he whispered, and he tipped a Pepsi can at us. "Got any pot?"

We shook our heads and apologized. He shrugged and moved on.

I had never thought much about what I expected to find in a Native village, but pot-smoking, bell-bottomed teenagers had certainly not been part of my picture. I knew, of course, that our wilderness trip had been artificial—plane transport, an airdrop of peanut butter and canned chicken, rubberized clothing, hauling ourselves up

cliffs for the fun of it. But I had also fashioned in my mind the existence of another world—a *real* one of hunting, gathering bark and
roots, splitting fish to dry, scrapping moose hides. I sometimes day-
dreamed myself into this country on the margin between wilderness
and civilization—a place where I might cut logs with a bowsaw or
chop a hole in a frozen river, sew moccasins beside a crackling woodstove while wolves howled on the next ridge. In such a world there
were no music tapes, painted fingernails, Pepsi cans, drugs.

At nineteen, I only sensed the irony. I wanted the life these young
Natives were rejecting; they wanted what I was convinced had absolutely no value. On the boardwalk, in my baggy backwoods clothes,
I was confused and disappointed. But I wondered: What came next
for these kids? How long could they cruise their boardwalk before it
wasn't enough? What life would they have here, where would they
go, what sort of place would they make for themselves in another
world?

We walked the boardwalk past more houses, outbuildings hung
with tools and wash basins, weed-circled snowmachines, a church,
a community hall with an open door and nothing inside except folding chairs and a cheap record player. A chained, blue-eyed husky
barked at us half-heartedly. Then the boardwalk came to an end,
giving way to a dirt trail that followed the edge of the bluff and, away
from the bluff, led to the hard ground of a volleyball court.

We looked down on the gray, slipping river. Already I felt nostal-
gia for it, for the sound of water rolling over sand, for the clean,
carved edges of the banks, for my own daydreams. Somewhere behind us, an outboard started up with a roar. We could still hear
music—the Doors now, a heavy, brooding rhythm.

"Think there's a ball?" someone asked, and we spread across the
court, looking among the weeds at the edges, finding only pop cans,
Snickers wrappers, part of a faded newspaper with an ad for mat-
tresses.

We walked back again the way we'd come, back to the airstrip. We
ate our last meal of cheese glop. We played the last hands of our
version of bridge, a game in which we made up the rules we didn't
know. I pressed two final wildflowers into the pages of my journal.
The sun fell behind the trees, but the air was still pale and warm, as
though the haze held the day's heat against the earth. We heard birds

settle into the trees, motors on the river. One by one, we went to the tents, zipped ourselves into sleep.

That's the truth of what happened, that summer of 1971. We emerged from the wilderness and found a village of acculturating Natives. For me, it made a melancholic end.

This story might well have ended there. There was, however, more.

I don't know what time it was when we woke. In the half-light inside our tent, I could see the tautness of the nylon ceiling, our boots piled by the door, Kathy lifting her head. None of us said anything at first. We were all registering: *gunshots*. They came from the direction of the village, a series of them, and then quiet, then a pounding noise, raised voices, more shots. I tried to convince myself it was some sort of celebration, firecrackers.

Gary slid around in his bag, grabbing clothes, pulling on pants. "I'll be right back," he said. Barefoot, T-shirt bunched over his shoulders, he unzipped the door, crouched his way out, zipped the door closed again. I sat partway up and watched mosquitoes hover and then reroost on the netting.

"Fuck," Kathy whispered.

We could hear the other tents unzip, Gary's low voice, and the others. There weren't any more shots. I wondered how far a random shot could travel. I wondered whether whoever was shooting would think about us and, if so, how hostile they might be. I remembered *Easy Rider*, when Peter Fonda and Dennis Hopper were beaten in their tent. We heard Gary come back, watched him crouch and enter. He slid back into his sleeping bag. "They've got the gun loaded," he said.

We'd hauled the bear gun, a 30.06, all through the mountains and down the river. We'd never needed to use it.

I noticed that Gary was leaving his clothes on.

"It was a long way away," Kathy said.

Whatever it was, it didn't have anything to do with us. I lay back down and closed my eyes. I listened to the river, saw it behind my eyes, that smooth, clear, imperturbable water, forever flowing. And then I was asleep again.

In the bright light of morning, the gunshots and voices were half-forgotten, as though dreamed. We gathered around our bowls of granola, curious in a vague sort of way, relieved that whatever it was had come to nothing as far as we were concerned. We would never know the reason for the shots and the uproar. Our plane was due. There was no time to go back to the village.

I walked down to the river to wash out my bowl. The river on the bend there was broad—twice as far across as I could throw a rock—and slow. A stalk of grass, caught in an eddy near the shore, followed itself around and around. I heard the sound of wings and, when I looked up, a kingfisher jerked past and disappeared into the trees on the opposite bank. I scooped water into my bowl, swished it around, poured the milky residue back into the river—and saw, behind me, a flash of gray-blue.

Startled, I spun around, nearly falling backward into the water. From behind a boulder, perhaps twenty feet away, a girl, still half-hidden, was watching me. I remembered her from the day before—one of the teenagers on the boardwalk. She wore the same tight jeans and gray-blue sweatshirt.

Her makeup had run, leaving dark smudges beneath her eyes, and her hair fell across her face in a tangle. I saw, though, that there was something wrong with her face. The ridge of her nose and one cheek were cut, streaked with blood.

I realized I was holding my plastic bowl in front of me like a shield. I lowered it to my side. "What happened?"

She edged a little more from behind the boulder, still leaning one hip against it as though she needed the support. I guessed she was about fifteen years old, but when she spoke, her voice was childlike, barely audible.

"They came back from fire fighting," she said.

I put my hand to my face, touched my nose. "Someone hurt you?"

"My brother," she said. "Everyone was drinking."

She stepped away from the boulder, but she was unsteady, swaying, and I understood she meant *everyone*. She was still drunk.

"Are you all right?" I asked, but she didn't answer. She had turned away and was walking toward the village, stiff-legged, lurching, but going there, not looking back at me.

A few years later, I moved to Alaska. By then, of course, I knew that people don't live in the wilderness, and I took a city-planning job in Anchorage. Anchoragites joke that their city is only a half-hour's drive from Alaska. I made that drive often, to the Chugach Mountains south of town. I hiked up Flattop or through Powerline Valley, and, though I never made it back to the Brooks Range, I was satisfied to know it was there, a day's flight north.

I married a man who designs warm houses and likes to cook. We moved to the edge of Anchorage, at the foot of the mountains, where we keep two dogs and a parrot. Moose wander through the yard and eat from the garden. When a new city administration decided I had planned enough bike paths and pocket parks, I switched to economic development. Now I work with hotel owners and ski resort builders, trying to encourage the tourism industry.

Thousands of Native people–Indian, Eskimo, Aleut–live in Anchorage. It is, in fact, sometimes called Alaska's largest Native village. There is a disproportionate number of Natives among the downtown drunks and the people served by our social agencies, but we prefer not to point this out. We choose instead to promote Native artwork–the ivory carvings, baskets, and fur-dressed dolls displayed in galleries and sold to tourists.

I read the newspapers. I read about suicides and murders in the villages, about the Native couple who accidently left their baby on a sandbar and couldn't find her when they remembered and went back, the young Native man who shot a woman in the head and then had sex with her dead body. I read the obituaries and know that the teenagers and young people aren't dying from disease and accidents, except as we understand alcoholism as a disease and the cause of despondency, drownings, freezings, fire, neglect, and violence.

The "problem" is not threatening, or even very visible, to most of us. In the villages and in Anchorage, the Natives prey on their own kind, destroy only themselves.

I give money to the United Way, to the soup kitchen and the detox center, and to an organization that buys plane tickets for stranded villagers who want to return home.

That story I told, about the summer of 1971? It's true. It happened, that girl on the beach with the cut face. But there was more.

That next morning, after the night of the gunshots, just as we were emerging from our tents and starting breakfast, children—maybe a dozen—arrived at our campsite. There was something slightly feral about them, the way they emerged from the brush—small, unwashed children in rumpled clothes, smelling of urine. Expressionless, they gathered around us, crowded elbow to elbow, and looked, not at us, but at a collapsed nylon tent and its aluminum skeleton, a pile of colored climbing slings and hardware, the featherweight stove roaring under a pot of water, our glut of high-tech equipment.

We tried to make conversation, to be friendly. What is your name? Is this your sister? What is her name? They answered in monosyllables, or not at all. I wasn't even sure if the younger ones spoke English, or if, until they started school, they knew only their Athabascan dialect.

"Cookies," one of the older boys said, his mouth twisting around the word.

Without discussion, we gave them our remaining Fig Newtons, a box of crackers, some dried banana chips, and a bag of nuts and raisins. I think we all understood that the children had not been fed that morning, that whatever had occurred in the village left them to their own devices. Yet there was about them no sense of panic, no expression of fear; whatever happened, I told myself, couldn't have been very bad.

The children took the food and started back the way they'd come. Partway across the field, nearly hidden from us behind grass and stalky weeds, they seemed, quietly, to divide and eat what we'd given them. And then they went on, disappearing from sight, back toward the village.

It was after that, after I'd eaten my granola, that I walked down to the river to rinse my bowl. I saw the girl there, and she told me about the drinking, and I watched her lurch away.

She said something before she left. She asked me to do something. What she said was, "Tell the bishop. Tell him Tina wants him to come. I need him to come here." Her makeup was smudged, blackening her eyes. I thought she must have been crying.

The plane came right after that, and we hurried to stuff our sleeping bags into their sacks and fold up the last tent. And then we were in Fairbanks, taking showers at the university, eating in a restaurant with fake-velvet wallpaper. I thought about the girl, but already she seemed impossibly distant. I had no idea what bishop she meant. I didn't know who to call, and besides, I wasn't near a phone, and we were in a hurry. I asked myself if it wasn't just an accident that we were even at the village, and I answered that what had happened had nothing to do with us. The situation would have been – would be – exactly the same if we'd never existed.

I didn't call, and I didn't even tell the others about the girl, and we drove on down the highway.

Today, when I left my office after work, I walked several blocks to meet my husband. I looked at some shoes in a window on Fifth Avenue and then cut past my favorite bookstore-cafe to wave at the owner and smell her espresso. Then I heard yelling.

Around the corner, in the middle of the street, a woman was stumbling, cursing and sobbing. She was a small woman, a Native, with uneven dark hair falling into her eyes and a paunchiness, front and back, beneath her loose clothes. Her denim seat was worn white.

A man, Native too, barrel-chested and with arms like tree trunks, was backing away from her. She ran at him, swinging, and her fist made a deadened thud against his arm.

Love. That's what she was yelling. *I love you,* and then a string of obscenities. Or maybe it was past tense – *loved.* She loved him or she had loved him. Her words slurred – something he did, something he didn't do, everything she'd done for him. She sobbed and threw herself against him like a cannonball.

"Leave me alone," he growled. "Get away from me." His voice fell flat, loaded with dismissal, disgust, contempt. The woman staggered backward, then erupted into a louder wailing, a more desperate rage, and ran at him again. The man shielded his face, tripped over the curb.

I wondered what I'd do if she managed to hurt him – or if he struck back. Other people walked slowly past, trying not to look, wondering the same thing, I was sure. This was, after all, not New York. We would intervene if the situation called for it.

The man was getting away. He backed behind a car and then jogged off. The woman beat the hood of the car, kicked a tire, lowered her head. People walking by picked up speed, continued on their errands. My chest felt tight, as though I'd been forgetting to breathe. And it came to me, what I had missed before.

I saw her again, Tina, in 1971, a flash of gray-blue in the corner of my eye, a teenager in a sweatshirt, with makeup and blood smeared on her face. I saw her lean from behind a boulder, then rest against the rock, heard her young voice, weak with what sounded like shame. "My brother hurt me." And then I saw her step clear of the boulder and sway. "Tell the bishop," she said. "Tell the bishop I need him to come here." I saw her walk away, unsteadily, head down, legs bowed.

I understood then what I couldn't have recognized at nineteen. Tina had been raped.

All those years since—who's to say they might not have brought Tina, with so many others, to the streets of Anchorage, locked into patterns of abuse?

The woman had given up kicking the car tire.

I opened my mouth, unsure of what I would say until the word came out. "Wait!" I called. The woman didn't look up. Other people glanced at me—this white woman in a long wool coat, with nylons and heels. Their looks were curious, disapproving. Perhaps they thought the car was mine. Perhaps they thought I was a social worker. I walked closer. The woman was leaning against the car now, pulling on her greasy hair, muttering. I could hear myself saying to Tina on the beach, *Did someone hurt you?* I placed my hand on the car's fender, a foot from where the woman leaned. She looked up, her face a pitted mask of hostility, a red-eyed hate.

I waited a minute, feeling the cool metal under my fingers, hearing the sounds of the city. And then—this is true, because I couldn't think of another possibility—I walked away.

Snowblind

Nadine flipped through the day's mail as she walked up the flight of stairs to her apartment. There, sandwiched among the usual sweepstakes offers and bills, was a plain white envelope with the familiar backward-slanting scribble. A letter! She squeezed the stack of mail, testing its solidness, preparing herself. Don't expect it to be much. Be ready to be disappointed, again.

Once inside her apartment, she dropped her purse on a chair, kicked off her shoes, and spread the mail on her kitchen counter. The letter's postmark was Barrow, Alaska. Christ, that was all the way at the top of the state—the coldest, remotest part. She turned the envelope over to check for a return address. No, nothing, none. There wouldn't be one inside either.

She left the letter sitting on the edge of the counter and went into the bedroom to change out of her work clothes. For a moment, she stood in front of the mirror, trying to see herself as someone else would. Thick around the waist, saggy buns. Winter fat hanging on into March.

She dropped her chin to see how it folded into her neck. That was how she looked at work, bent over her papers or leaning into the phone. A typical Washington career woman, she supposed, heading already for middle age. The only atypical thing about her was this—this—what was it?—relationship?—with Eric.

It had been a long time since she'd heard from him. He'd phoned in November from some kind of barge, through a radio system where they both had to say *over* every time they finished speaking. An engine chugged in the background. "Cook Inlet," he'd shouted, and something about pan ice and anchor ice. Before that, the previous August, he'd sent a piece of smoked salmon with a greasy letter-will-follow note. She'd known better than to hold her breath; no letter had followed, until now.

Nadine put the tea kettle on the stove and opened her other mail. When there was nothing left except Eric's letter, she studied the penciling of her name and address, picturing his hand shaping the letters, fingers curled around as though he were writing upside down. She remembered, when he was in Washington three years earlier, how tan his hands had been, how blond the hairs on the back of them. In Barrow, sunless, his hand would have grown pale, the hair darker. She pressed the envelope down against the counter. It was a small, cheap dime-store envelope; she could see lined paper inside, and words, folded into each other. She ripped it open.

The note was on a scrap of paper, a third of a sheet torn from a spiral notebook. *I lost the letter I wrote you,* it said, *but since I already had the envelope, I'm mailing it anyway. The letter didn't say much. Typed it (touch) while I was incapacitated from snow blindness. I'm starting a dog team. Gee! Haw! XXX*

Nadine's hands shook as she folded the paper and tucked it back into the envelope. So much waiting, so much longing, and then this—just this handful of hints. Snowblind! He'd been hurt, endangered, in pain, and she hadn't even known. She imagined him, after his rescue, lying quietly on a cot in some village clinic, patches covering his eyes. Then, with eyes still bandaged, he'd somehow typed out a lettter to her. And then lost it. But was he all better now? What had the letter told?

Of course, losing the letter was right in character for Eric. At work, his desk had always been cluttered, important papers mislaid. She remembered him searching for a memo he wanted to show her, moving one stack of paper and then another, all the while saying "I know it's here somewhere" but looking like he had no hope of finding it and, in fact, not finding it. The papers on his desk, she'd noticed, were mostly the kinds of things—press releases and meeting notices—everyone else deposited immediately into their wastebaskets. Newspapers, yellowing along their edges, were mixed in among them, forgotten, or hoarded, as though he thought he might someday need them, perhaps to start a fire.

That forgetfulness and disorder were all part of who he was and what had, in fact, charmed her. Each time he left her apartment, she was sure to find something he'd forgotten—a pocketful of change, a wristwatch she'd never seen him wear, a pound of butter. Once, she found his T-shirt—black, with a faded yellow sun and the words *Howling Dog*—with her clothes. It had a cluster of holes on one side, as though it had been spattered with battery acid or chewed by a small animal. She slept in it for a week before washing it, and she never did give it back.

Nadine turned off her tea water and poured herself a glass of wine instead. Sinking into her sofa, she repeated Eric's few scrawled words. *I lost the letter . . . didn't say much.* She pictured him loping down a hallway, wearing his scuffed basketball shoes and a gaudy pink tie, drawing looks of disapproval and not noticing, or not caring.

The first time she'd noticed him enough to wonder about him, she'd been having dinner with her friend Susan. Susan made a face. "That guy's always so messy," she said, and Nadine turned to see who she was watching.

She knew he worked in the Alaskan congressional office—she'd seen him on the Hill—and he *was* messy. Even now, in a nice restaurant, his straw-colored hair was standing up as though he'd just pulled clothes over his head. His untrimmed beard bushed out around the top of his sweater, a too-small one with sleeves that stopped inches short of his wrists. He sprawled in his chair, legs stretched under the table, like a teenager who hadn't been taught to sit up and show some manners. Not too impressive, Nadine thought, for a guy who must be at least thirty.

It surprised her, then, to see who was with him. The woman was tall and slim, Scandinavian-looking, with fair skin and a cap of straight blond hair. She wore a stylish brown suit with a silk blouse. When she laughed at something Eric said, her teeth flashed white. She was certainly the best-looking woman in the restaurant, the kind of woman Nadine felt intimidated by. "Who's that woman?" she asked Susan.

"I think his girlfriend," Susan said. "I've seen them together before. Don't you wonder what she sees in him?"

Their food came and they turned their talk to other things, but afterward Nadine took more notice of Eric at work. She'd see him bouncing down the hall with his shirttail out or slumping in the back of a committee hearing, staring absentmindedly out a window and making notes on the side of his hand while everyone around him scribbled onto legal pads. She liked the fact that he was there, a sort of counterpoint to the seriousness and self-importance of those around him.

Then one day Eric stood beside her desk, asking her a question about veterans' benefits because, he explained, "I'm told you know all about this stuff." In fact, Nadine knew what he needed to know, but so did a lot of other people. After that, he often came by or called when he needed to find out something, and she could usually help him. He was so innocent about politics and bureaucracy, she found herself feeling sorry for him. On the other hand, he was obviously very bright; he asked questions that cut to the heart of issues and was quick to grasp whatever she told him. His undisguised skepticism about government reminded her of how inured to its shortcomings the rest of them were.

One Sunday that spring, Nadine was walking toward her apartment when she heard her name called. It was Eric, running to catch up. He said he was looking for cherry trees. There weren't any in Nadine's neighborhood. When they reached her building she pointed him off toward a park.

A week later he showed up at her door on his own, his beard littered with the reddish husks of budding trees, his jeans ripped out in the knees as though he'd climbed mountains to get there. She'd had to invite him in.

They sat drinking beer and he talked about Alaska. Nadine had known other people from Alaska; they all talked about it being the biggest, greatest, and newest—worse than Texans, those Alaskans. But Eric was the first to tell her details of Alaskan life; he described fishing for salmon from a pitching boat, cleaning a whale's bones and wiring them back together, building a log cabin in the woods. The way he talked about these things, matter-of-factly – they seemed as commonplace to him as pages of the Congressional Record and the workings of word processors and copying machines were to her.

He paced her small living room, like a caged bear or someone who had recently given up smoking, full of nervous energy. "It used to be," he said, "Alaska was the place you could go and do anything. You wanted to build a cabin – you just knocked down some trees and did it. You wanted to eat – you put out a net for some fish and shot a moose." He frowned, and she noticed how dark the green in his eyes was – like moss growing in the shade, she thought, matching him with his Alaskan woods. "It's really too bad. Some of us need Alaska, even if it's only in our minds. You know, even if *we're* not there, we need *Alaska* to be there."

Nadine had heard that argument before. Whenever people wanted to preserve wild areas, they said it was because it was important that there be such places, even if no one even went there. It seemed logical to her. She'd been camping in the Smokies, years before, and she'd visited Cape Cod and seen thousands of shorebirds. She'd never wanted to go to Alaska, but she loved the idea that it was up there. "So that's why you're here," she said.

"Why?"

"To do what you can to preserve Alaska."

"Hell, no." Eric sat down and took another swallow of beer. "Government isn't going to save Alaska. Government just makes more regulations and paperwork." He sucked one end of his moustache.

"If you don't believe in government solving problems," Nadine persisted, "then why are you here?"

"My wife wanted to finish her degree at Georgetown," he said. "Also, I needed a grubstake."

"Grubstake?" she asked, thinking *wife?* That woman's his wife, and he comes *here* to tell me about Alaska?

"Money," he said and drank the rest of his beer.

He came another time, in out of the rain, his hair stuck to the sides of his head, and told her about the crevasse he once fell into on a glacier, how blue the ice was, and that there really were such things as ice worms. He told about a grizzly bear he'd come face to face with in the woods. "You can't outrun a bear," he deadpanned, "but that's okay. You just need to be able to outrun one of the people you're with."

He was eating cashews from a bowl on her coffee table. When he finished them he jumped up. "I've got to go." She got up too and he grabbed her, giving her a quick hug and a kiss on the mouth. It was all so natural, she felt as though he'd just gulped his breakfast and was rushing to work, kissing his wife on the way out the door. Then he was gone, and she realized she had never before kissed a man with a shaggy moustache and beard. He'd smelled like nuts and something else—his sweater, wet wool, smoke, as though he'd just been sitting beside a campfire, drying out.

When he came again, he brought her a book—a dog-eared collection of Alaskan stories by a friend of his. "There's a particularly good one," he said, ruffling pages. "It's about cabin fever—you know, the guy who spends too much time in the bush without seeing anyone and goes nuts. You'll like it."

She started to ask him why he thought she in particular would like a story about someone going crazy, but he took her hand and drew her across the kitchen to him. He kissed her, this time as though he meant it. Nadine turned her head and pushed him away. It surprised her to see *him* looking surprised and a little hurt.

"Well, what do you think?" she said. "You've already told me that you're married." She didn't tell him that he was wild-eyed, with newspaper ink smudged on his forehead.

"Jessie's gone back to Alaska," he said.

So that was it. No wonder he'd wolfed down all her crackers and cheese as though they were all the dinner he'd had that night. She leaned against the counter and crossed her arms. He stared at her, still so surprised and wounded-looking that she had to laugh. She pushed him out the door, but her hands gripped the back of his shirt with a fierceness that scared her; they didn't want to let go.

The next time he stood in her living room with a sharp elbow sticking through a hole in his shirt, having just demonstrated how a porcupine swats its tail in defense (she'd displayed her wildlife ignorance by saying she thought porcupines shot their quills), she dropped the last of her resistence. He wrapped his arms around her and no longer seemed so awkward and ill-mannered. When he kissed her, she breathed his smell—that woodsy, wild animal smell—

and she imagined Alaskan winds blowing through forests and across mountains. And rivers – she imagined ice melting, water feeding into rivers, flooding.

When he was gone, she tried to explain it to herself. It wasn't love, exactly. She didn't really mind that he had a wife. It wasn't sex, although sex was a part of it. It had something to do with charm – not the type taught at charm school but something deeper, more primitive.

Or maybe it *was* love – a kind of love.

And a little bit, she admitted – a little bit had to be flattery, because now that his terrific-looking wife was away, *she* – plain and ordinary, un-Alaskan Nadine – was his choice.

And so, although she still dated other men and continued as usual with her public life, Nadine let Eric's visits become a pattern with her. The usual parties were unusually dull; she suffered through the political talk of intense young men as alike as their suits and power ties. Leaving early, she waited at home, listening eagerly for his knock. When he was with her, she might have been on one of his glowing mountaintops. And when he was gone, she wrapped herself in her sheets, holding on, through her sleep, to his smell.

One evening, Eric sat at her kitchen table and drew log cabin notches on the back cover of a report she'd brought home to read. "This is a round notch," he said. "This is a saddle notch." He darkened the cutaway portion of the round notch with the pencil. "This is the strongest and most weather-resistent. You can see how water would get in the saddle notches and rot your walls."

Nadine wondered what someone, picking the report off her shelf at work, would make of the drawings. Eric drew another set. "This is a dovetail."

"How did you learn all this?" Nadine asked. "How did you learn to build log cabins?"

Eric shrugged. "It's something you learn when you live in Alaska."

Nadine was used to Eric's habit of talking about Alaska without talking about himself, although she hadn't decided why he was like that. Sometimes she thought he just forgot that she didn't already know all about him. Other times, she thought he couldn't talk about himself without mentioning his wife – and he didn't like to do that. When they talked, it was as though Jessie didn't exist, and

Nadine tried not to be curious about the sort of woman who would be Eric's wife.

"Well," she said, "you still never told me how you came to live in Alaska."

"I just went there," he said. "It was where I wanted to be."

"How old were you?" she asked.

"Nineteen."

"And what about your parents? Do you have some?"

"Yes," he said, but he didn't tell her about them.

She kept asking. "Where are you from originally?"

His eyes opened wide. "Planet Earth. I'm a wanderer."

Another night, as he rose to leave, she put out a hand to stop him. "What's the rush?" she said. "Can't you stay?"

"It's late," he said, looking around the room for a clock, finally knocking over the one beside the bed. "I've got to get home."

"But why?" she said.

"Jessie," he said, giving her a curious look. "My wife. Remember? I have one."

Of course. But he'd never told her she was back. "I thought she was in Alaska."

"She's back." He was buttoning his shirt. "I thought you knew. She's been back a long time."

Nadine watched him pull his socks over his long, knobby feet. She remembered Jessie as she'd seen her in the restaurant—slim, blond, smiling. She was back, and still he came to her.

Nadine settled into the couch with her third glass of wine. She read the note again. *I lost the letter I wrote you . . . I was incapacitated by snow blindness . . . XXX.* She looked at the words, one by one, trying to read what might lie behind them. They'd been written quickly, dashed off. She saw Eric with a dogsled, leaning against the back of it and gripping a pencil through thick gloves, his dogs yapping and straining in their harnesses. What else had he thought and not written? What had the real letter told? What if someone else found it? She imagined someone catching the paper as it blew across the tundra; someone picking it up, rumpled and smeared with ketchup, from a booth in a roadhouse; someone opening to it in a library book; Jessie, finding it under dirty socks?

He'd left so suddenly that August, at the beginning of the congressional recess. He just quit and left—one day tossing out all the papers he'd accumulated on his desk for so long. The same evening he stopped by, distracted, his head already back in Alaska, to tell her about a canoe trip he was planning. The next morning he caught a plane before she was even awake.

Letters and cards had arrived sporadically, short on personal details but postmarked from all over Alaska. They were often tattered and grimy, as though they'd been carried by dogsled, canoe, and trained falcon over mountains and oceans to reach the nearest post office. One, folded several times, was smudged with mud and what Nadine took to be fish blood. Another, a postcard of Mount McKinley, was wrinkled, with blurred writing, as though it had sat out in the rain. Anchorage, Bethel, Sand Point, Seldovia—some of them places she'd never heard of. *Caught a salmon sixty-two pounds. Potatoes here as big as double fists. Finally got some insulation in the ceiling.* (What ceiling? Where did he live? He never said.) *Wood splits pretty good at forty below, but I frostbit the end of my nose.*

Nadine was enchanted by these sketchy details of his real life. The man who couldn't find a pencil on his desk seemed to be all over Alaska, doing everything that that environment demanded. If he was lost in Washington, back in Alaska he was clearly flourishing.

His scattered words were never enough but, given Eric, Nadine was impressed that he managed to get letters to her at all. That he continued to remember her address and to actually find paper and stamps and get the letters posted seemed a remarkable feat.

He never gave her a return address. She assumed that, despite his wanderings, he lived someplace with Jessie, but that he didn't want her to write to him there. So, without expecting or allowing a reply, he kept his letters coming—maybe twice in one month and then not again for six months. That was something. What, she didn't know.

Occasionally Eric called, usually in the middle of the night, as though he didn't remember the four-hour difference. Often there was some kind of background noise, his voice straining against music and laughter. "Where are you?" she always asked as soon as the dozen or so coins finished their fall through the phone's pay mechanism. It might be anywhere – the only phone in an Indian village, a roadhouse "somewhere on the highway." Once he said "Alaskaland," and she conjured up a vision of an Alaskan Disneyland, then wondered if it was just one of his names for Alaska, the way he sometimes spoke the postal abbreviation "A-K."

"Alaskaland?" she said. "Is that a real place?"

"It's in Fairbanks. It's kind of a tourist place. There's a zoo, and they've got demonstrations of stuff like gold panning." She heard another man's voice say "C'mon, we gotta go" and Eric answer "Yeah, just a minute, I need to make this call." Then he told her about a fish-cleaning competition he'd just watched. "The Indian guy with the knife beat all the Eskimo women with ulus."

Each time it was as though that precise moment – a stop on the way somewhere or unexpected proximity to an empty phone booth – was the only, or best, time he could find to call. It was always too quick, barely long enough to establish each other's existence and general welfare, and then nothing – silence – for months more.

Nadine, sipping her wine, thought of her desk at work, how it sat in the same spot day after day, her black fine-tipped pens aligned in her drawer. Her appointment calendar was marked off in fifteen-minute segments; her push-button phone had half a dozen lines and an automatic call-back provision. Here at home, the same four walls surrounded her every night. She could open her refrigerator and find green apples in the crisper. It was the life she expected to have – ordered, productive, professionally satisfying. Meanwhile, there Eric was in Barrow, Alaska. She could see him, bundled in parkas and fur mittens, disappearing down a snow-covered trail behind a team of huskies. He'd be warming a log cabin with a woodfire, throwing a slab of frozen meat (moose? caribou?) on the stove to thaw. And summers – there he was, careening down a wild river in a canoe, hooking fish, thinking of her, stopping at a remote village to post a letter. Alaska, all of it, fit around him like the background of a photograph.

Nadine tried to picture herself, riding through the wilderness on the back of a sled or, even, bundled in furs in the basket of one. She liked the *idea* of it, but she knew it wasn't something she would ever do in real life. She could just barely see herself climbing through summertime fields of Alaskan flowers.

However tiny the trace of wildness in her city soul, Eric must have found it. Something had made him think she had the ability to kick off her high heels and step into those giant white "bunny boots" he said everyone wore in the Arctic. He had even said, while he was still in Washington and later, on the phone, that she would come to Alaska some day. He wasn't inviting her; he stated it as a fact, as though someday she would get on the wrong plane to New York and step off in Anchorage. She remembered saying "It's not exactly on the way to anywhere."

She lifted her glass in a toast. Here's to Eric—messy, disorganized, unconstrained Eric, with ink spots in all his pockets from pens he forgot to cap. And here—she lifted the glass again—here's to Alaska, where there's still room for being anyone and doing anything, where you could probably live your whole life without owning a pen or reading a government report.

Life did go on. After her one wine-drunk evening, Nadine got up the next morning, put the envelope and its note away in a drawer, and went to work. Eric stayed in her mind, distracting her enough that she sat through an entire hearing on health care cost containment without paying enough attention to figure out what the proposed plan entailed. The next day he was a little less with her, and the day after a little less than that. Still, there was never a day when he slipped out of her thoughts altogether; at any moment his bearded face, his irreverent grin, would break through, leaving her with the old ache.

Weeks passed into months without another word from him. She pictured him shedding his winter furs and then, on a river again, growing tan, with sunstreaks through his hair. She knew that any day she'd find a smudged letter in her box, or some night the phone would ring, rousing her from sleep. Every evening her step quickened as she closed in on her mailbox. Every night she held herself on the edge of sleep, ready to wake for his call.

One day in July, Nadine stopped in a bookstore to buy a birthday card for her nephew. As she approached the counter with the card, she noticed a woman browsing through the rack of new paperbacks. Even after so much time, Nadine was sure she didn't mistake her. She hadn't changed; she was as lithe, blond, and smartly dressed as that time she'd seen her in the restaurant. Nadine hesitated only a second before walking up to her. "Aren't you Jessie?"

The woman nodded. Her face, open and expectant, had that look of trust that city people so seldom wore.

"I used to work with Eric." Nadine tried to sound casual. "What's he doing these days?" It occurred to her that they might be separated. Eric, after all, never mentioned her in his three years of letters—and how many people these days stayed married that long? "Last I heard, someone said he was racing sled dogs."

Jessie laughed. "The rumor mill—isn't it wonderful? Actually, Eric *did* have a dog for a while. Someone gave him a cull from a team, but she got hit by a car."

Nadine could see the words of his note, stenciled precisely into her memory. *I'm starting a dog team.* She made herself laugh too, and then stopped abruptly. "Oh, but I'm sorry about the dog."

Jessie shrugged. "Well, she shouldn't have been running loose. We live in downtown Anchorage, which isn't the best place for dogs."

"Didn't he—didn't Eric also have a case of snow blindness last winter? Is he all better?"

"Oh, yes," Jessie smiled. "It wasn't that bad. We went skiing one day, and he forgot his sunglasses. It's like sunburn—you don't really know you're getting it until it's too late. The next day he felt obliged to lie around with his eyes closed, letting me wait on him, but then he was okay."

Nadine felt embarrassed. Why had she pictured him struggling, blinded, through the wilderness when, of course, Jessie was there to take care of him?

"What's Eric doing?" Jessie said, repeating Nadine's question. "He mostly works for my brother, building condos in Anchorage. That and some government jobs—tank farms, public safety buildings—around the state. But of course, now we're here."

Nadine tried hard not to show her surprise. She mentally knocked back the pitch of her voice before she spoke. "You mean Eric's in town too?"

"We're visiting his parents. You know, they live in Arlington," Jessie said, as though anyone who knew Eric even casually would know *that*. "Eric grew up here."

Nadine forced a smile; she felt sweat sticking in her armpits. "Well, I should get going." She nodded her head in what she hoped was a friendly expression and headed for the counter.

"What was your name?" Jessie called after her.

For a second, Nadine thought she would make up a name, but by the time she opened her mouth the opportunity was gone. "Nadine Andrews," she said, keeping eye contact just long enough to see that it didn't draw a reaction.

"I'll tell Eric you asked for him," she heard Jessie say.

Outside the store, the noon sun bore down on the pavement. Nadine lifted a hand to shade her eyes and remembered again her alarm over Eric's snow blindness. Had he really been typing out a letter to her while Jessie brought him cold drinks and adjusted pillows behind him? Had he honestly hoped to put together a dog team? And why had he never mentioned his construction work? Construction of government facilities, for God's sake!

She moved into the crush of workers returning from their lunches. Eric, just miles away, not even in Alaska. An ordinary, forgetful, perhaps even dishonest man. It wasn't anger she felt as much as sorrow, a sharper point to the normal spike of disappointment. If Eric wasn't that different—special—and if Alaska, with its busy streets and condos, wasn't either, then how could she—or she and Eric—be?

And she remembered again, what he had said, pacing like a bear, across her living room, that first time. *Some of us need Alaska, even if it's only in our minds.*

For Eric, maybe it *was* all in his mind.

And she was still in Washington, setting her feet down, one after the other, on the hard sidewalk. Swept along by the crowd, Nadine gradually adjusted her eyes to the glare.

Why I Live at the
Natural History Museum

I was getting along fine. After I moved to Alaska, I lived a quiet life with my cat, my hermit crab, and my ant colony, in a small house not far from the beach. The main social functions in town were bingo at the Community Center and hobnobbing in front of the post office. Most of the time I stayed home with the cat, the crab, and the ant colony, and we waited for earthquakes. Oh, two or three times a week I went into the Natural History Museum and took care of things there. I dusted the cases and typed new labels and showed people around, if anyone came in.

My children were grown. Alice left home at an early age and had been all over the Lower Forty-Eight on a motorcycle. I never expected to see her in Alaska. I didn't think there were enough paved roads. Glenn lived with his father after we were divorced. We were strangers to one another.

That's what he said when he arrived on my doorstep. "We shouldn't be strangers," he said. "I'd like to get to know you." He moved into my hobby room. His friends stayed in the living room, wrapped in my afghans and quilts. They were always shivering, and their noses ran.

Alice and her husband were already in the guest room. They'd arrived just days before. "I'm pregnant," Alice had announced with a yard-wide smile. She didn't have to tell me; I could see that she had her coat unbuttoned from the bottom, making room. She had decided to quit the road and settle down. "I'm ready to nest," she said. She took the television into the guest room and stayed there. Her husband went out for beer. I think his name was Rudy. He never said anything to me, except when I asked him where he was from. Montrose, he said. I still don't know what state that is.

Bruni was the first to complain. Bruni is a fastidious cat, very clean, very neat, very set in her ways. She puts up with my little projects – the necklaces and bookmarks I make from sea shells and pressed flowers – but she doesn't like a lot of disturbance. She didn't like being closed out of the guest room, where she was used to enjoying the warmth of the late afternoon sun as it crossed the foot of the bed. She followed me around, protesting loudly. She was barely mollified when I took her in my lap and adjusted the floor lamp to warm her. Then, the night Glenn moved in, her panic-stricken cries woke me. Her kitty box was behind the hobby room door, and she needed it.

I opened the door for her. The room was stuffy, with a smell like smoke and dirty socks. In the light from the hall, I looked at Glenn's sleeping form where it lay wrapped in a sleeping bag under my worktable. The bag was old Army issue, too hot for indoors, and he had it unzipped and open around his bare shoulders. His face was buried in a balled-up, gray T-shirt. He didn't look like anyone I had ever known, although I supposed he was a nice boy.

Bruni scratched over her business, and we left. The next day I moved her litter box into my room.

The ants would have complained, if ants could complain. The ones that survived, I know they were angry. I could see it in the way they moved afterward – abruptly, with their pinchers open, without forgiveness. They had worked so hard and so long to create their civilization of tunnels and chambers. We had suffered two recent earthquakes with minor damage to the colony, nothing that couldn't be cleaned up in a day. And then – a big 10 on the Richter scale.

The ant farm was in the living room. One noon, after the boys were gone, I stepped around their piles of bedding and a line of tape players to feed my ants. The colony was in chaos. It looked as though someone had shaken the farm upside down and sideways until everything was caved in, until it was all just rubble with ants buried, crushed, spun on their heads. Those who weren't killed or crippled were trying to dig out, grain of dirt by grain of dirt.

I took the farm into my room and sat there with Bruni and the ants and the crab. The crab, Hermie, lived in a glass aquarium full of sand and rocks beside the window. He was tucked into his shell, the end of his large claw hanging out.

From the other room, the guest room, I could hear the "Wheel of Fortune" wheel turning.

"Well, friends," I told them. "I'll have to say something." Bruni stopped rumbling and widened her yellow eyes. I think she didn't believe me.

That night I put my foot down.

I started with Alice. "Alice," I said through the door, "I need to talk to you."

"Just a minute," she shouted. I could hear her talking to Rudy, and he said something back, and then drawers were opened and shut. They sounded like they were getting dressed. They asked me in, finally.

They were both in bed, with pillows behind them and the covers pulled up across their bellies. Rudy's belly was almost as big as Alice's. Alice was wearing an ivory silk blouse. It was mine, my best. The clothes I seldom wore, except for special occasions, I kept in the guest-room closet. Rudy wasn't wearing any shirt at all. His chest was matted with dark hair.

"Yes?" Alice said. Her voice was high-pitched and faint, as though she was pretending to not be well.

I moved a stack of dirty plates from the chair and sat down. The television was still on—a furniture commercial. Alice and Rudy were both watching it. I remembered that "Upstairs, Downstairs" was on that evening. It was my favorite, and I never missed it. I never *had* missed it. I looked around the room. My belongings were gone from the windowsill, replaced with more dirty dishes, motorcycle helmets, and what might have been articles of underwear.

"You've rearranged," I said.

They both looked at me and smiled.

I wanted to kick myself for not thinking of my beach treasures sooner. I tried to remember everything I'd had on the sill: dozens of agates and pieces of jade, snail fossils, a tooth from a beluga whale, dried cottongrass, and feathers of all kinds. I was particularly proud of my bouquet of eagle wing feathers, with their sharp edges. I was afraid to ask where everything had gone to.

"I had a few things on the windowsill," I said. "I hope they weren't in your way."

"Dead things," Alice said. "Real attractive."

Rudy pointed into the corner, at a paper bag. There were two crumpled and twisted beer cans on top, but I recognized the piece of driftwood sticking out past them. It was part of my arrangement.

"I'll move them in a minute," I said.

"These Alaskan ads are a riot," Alice said. "Can you get cable here?"

"I'm afraid not."

She shrugged without taking her eyes from the screen. "Such is life."

"Tell her that joke," Rudy said.

"What joke?"

"The one about life."

"That's not a joke."

"Tell it anyway."

Alice sighed. "Life is a bitch and then you die. See, it's not a joke." I didn't think so either.

A new show started. It was a cop show, and Alice and Rudy knew all the characters. I began to wonder how they'd watched so much television if they were always riding around on motorcycles. Alice commented some more about what a "weenie" one of the cops was, and I realized that they thought I'd come into their room to watch television with them and enjoy their company. I waited for the next commercial.

"I won't stay," I said. "I was just wondering, how long are you planning to visit?"

They both looked at me again. I recognized the expression on Alice's face. It was the same look of disbelief she'd worn as a child when I'd told her she couldn't cross the highway, couldn't stay out all night, couldn't hitchhike to Mardi Gras. She looked as though I'd forgotten something, and what I'd forgotten was that Alice always did exactly what she wanted.

"Visit?" she said. "But this is my *home*. You're my *mother*. And I'm going to have a *baby*." She thrust out her belly as if to prove it, and I thought she might have the baby right then, just to show me she could.

Rudy put an arm around Alice and hugged her.

I took my bag of rocks and feathers to my own room, stopping along the way to dump the beer cans in the kitchen trash. As I swung back through the living room, I noticed that half the tape players were gone, but they'd been replaced with three televisions. I took one into my room. Those boys! I could almost forgive them for putting out their cigarettes in my aloe vera's pot.

The Natural History Museum is in the basement of the Community Center. It's run by volunteers who share an interest in the flora and fauna of the area. People like myself. We have a rock display, an exhibit of clamshells showing all the kinds you can dig locally, mounted salmon and trout, and stuffed animals. Taxidermied animals, that is. A moose's head, a dall sheep's head, a whole black bear cub, a beaver set up to look like it's chewing a tree. We have quite a few stuffed ducks and a rough-legged hawk and even some songbirds. The smaller birds look particularly moth-eaten.

We have lots of bones. We've got skeletons of a sea lion and an eagle that volunteers pieced together. We've got whale vertebrae and the disks, as big as turkey platters, that fit between them. We've got a table covered with skulls–porpoise, sea lion, seal, bear, moose, wolf, coyote, dog, marmot, porcupine, weasel, and a lot more. We even have a human skull. That's the question I get asked most often; where did we get the human skull? I don't know. It was donated. I expect someone found it on the beach after it eroded from a burial. It would be from an Indian or Eskimo, a long time ago.

Most of the time, it's very quiet at the museum. The only sound is the click of the typewriter keys as I type new labels for things. Someone who typed labels before me didn't know the difference between *its* and *it's,* so I have all those to correct. Or I rearrange displays and make new labels to explain them.

On Tuesday, I found a good specimen of a sea urchin in the storeroom. I matched it with a photo of a living one and put the pair on display next to the clams. Then I typed up a card giving the pertinent information and explaining that sea urchin gonads were an important part of the diet of the Aleut people. After that I worked with our starfish, organizing them into families and turning a couple over so people could see the mouths and the podia. Feet, that is.

You can see that there's no end to what can be done at the museum.

During the day, three people came in. That's about three more than we usually have for visitors. The first one was a Native lady looking for bingo. She had the wrong day and the wrong time, both, as well as the wrong part of the building. Usually when people come in accidentally like that, they stay to look around, but she didn't. Maybe she'd seen it all before.

After school, two boys about ten years old came in. They needed to do some kind of report for school, they told me. They sat at the table and drew pictures of the skulls. They were so quiet, I hardly knew they were there. When I walked by I noticed that one of them was embellishing with crossbones, fighter jets, and swastikas. They left soon after that, but not before they'd wiggled the wolf's teeth to see if any of them would come loose.

That evening, when I got home, Glenn was wearing my bathrobe and shower cap, and the house smelled like gasoline. The hall was full of motorcycle parts. I went straight to my room and curled up on the bed with Bruni. Music, very heavy on the bass, pounded through from the guest room. I knew the ants were feeling it like tremors. Bruni crossed her eyes as though she had a headache.

"They're my own children," I told her.

Something smashed in the back of the house. I wondered if the bathroom sink might have come off the wall. It sounded that heavy.

"Perhaps I wasn't the best mother," I said.

The doorbell rang. I heard arguing, and then a door slammed.

"I didn't teach them to be quiet and polite and to appreciate Nature."

Someone turned the music up louder. Bruni flung herself about, scratching at the air and spitting.

"I see what you mean," I said. "Yes, there's only one thing to do."

I carried her out to my car, then made two more trips for Hermie, the ants, my flower press, a suitcase, and my pillow. I didn't see

Glenn or Alice or Rudy. One of Glenn's friends was in the kitchen, weighing something on a scale. If there hadn't been so much noise I would have told him that we had a scale just like that down at the museum, as part of our gold-mining exhibit.

So now I live at the Natural History Museum. Bruni likes stalking the dustballs under the storage cases, and Hermie's actually on display with a label telling how hermit crabs make their homes in empty snail shells. I keep the ant farm next to the cot in the backroom, and I watch their steady progress. It won't be long before they've rebuilt their basic chambers and connecting tunnels.

All of us appreciate the peace and quiet.

I've got an idea, though. I've always liked our skeletons—the sea lion and the eagle. I've wanted to do a project like that myself. The problem is, you don't just find whole skeletons sitting around in the wild; the bones get scattered. To put together a skeleton, you have to start with the whole dead animal.

It just happens that we have several whole dead animals in the museum's freezer. People bring them to us, and we keep them frozen until we eventually get them stuffed or made into skeletons. From the inventory list I know we have a sandhill crane, lots of small birds that died flying into people's windows, a red fox, a newborn moose, two weasels, crabs, and a shark. I also know that we have a baby seal that's already been flensed. All that needs to be done is to boil it up in a big pot, to cook the rest of the meat off the bones. Then I can piece the vertebrae, the ribs, and the long bones back together. I have just the place to exhibit it, next to the sea lion, where people can make anatomical comparisons.

The key to this plan is having a place to do the boiling. In the past we used the kitchen upstairs in the Community Center, but everyone complained of the smell. In fact, they had to cancel bingo. It's a rotten smell.

That's why I'll take it home to do in my kitchen.

If that doesn't clear out the house, I'll do a whale. We have a minke whale stored down at the impound yard, getting picked at by birds and animals. The smell carries for three blocks. It's just about ready to fall apart into boiling-size pieces.